The Borrowers

MARY NORTON

Published by Paperview Ltd. (2005)
www.paperviewgroup.com

ISBN: 2-87427-149-7

CHAPTER ONE

It was Mrs May who first told me about them. No, not me.
How could it have been me—a wild, untidy, self-willed little
girl who stared with angry eyes and was said to crunch her
teeth? Kate, she should have been called. Yes, that was it—
Kate. Not that the name matters much either way: she barely
comes into the story.

Mrs May lived in two rooms in Kate's parents' house in
London; she was, I think, some kind of relation. Her bedroom was on the first floor, and her sitting-room was a room
which, as part of the house, was called 'the breakfast-room'.
Now breakfast-rooms are all right in the morning when the
sun streams in on the toast and marmalade, but by afternoon
they seem to vanish a little and to fill with a strange silvery
light, their own twilight; there is a kind of sadness in them
then, but as a child it was a sadness Kate liked. She would
creep in to Mrs May just before tea-time and Mrs May would
teach her to crochet.

Mrs May was old, her joints were stiff, and she was—not
strict exactly, but she had that inner certainty which does
instead. Kate was never 'wild' with Mrs May, nor untidy, nor
self-willed; and Mrs May taught her many things besides crochet: how to wind wool into an eggshaped ball; how to run-

and-fell and plan a darn; how to tidy a drawer and to lay, like a blessing, above the contents, a sheet of rustling tissue against the dust.

'Why so quiet, child?' asked Mrs May one day, when Kate was sitting hunched and idle upon the hassock. 'What's the matter with you? Have you lost your tongue?'

'No,' said Kate, pulling at her shoe button, 'I've lost the crochet hook...' (they were making a bed-quilt—in woollen squares: there were thirty still to do), 'I know where I put it,' she went on hastily; 'I put it on the bottom shelf of the book case just beside my bed.'

'On the bottom shelf?' repeated Mrs May, her own needle flicking steadily in the firelight. 'Near the floor?'

'Yes,' said Kate, 'but I looked on the floor. Under the rug. Everywhere. The wool was still there though. Just where I'd left it.'

'Oh dear,' exclaimed Mrs May lightly, 'don't say they're in this house too!'

'That what are?' asked Kate.

'The Borrowers,' said Mrs May, and in the half-light she seemed to smile.

Kate stared a little fearfully. 'Are there such things?' she asked after a moment.

'As what?'

Kate blinked her eyelids. 'As people, other people, living in a house who... borrow things?'

Mrs May laid down her work. 'What do you think?' she

asked.

'I don't know,' said Kate, looking away and pulling hard at her shoe button. 'There can't be. And yet'—she raised her head—'and yet sometimes I think there must be.'

'Why do you think there must be?' asked Mrs May.

'Because of all the things that disappear. Safety-pins, for instance. Factories go on making safety-pins, and every day people go on buying safety-pins and yet, somehow, there never is a safety-pin just when you want one. Where are they all? Now, at this minute? Where do they go to? Take needles,' she went on. 'All the needles my mother ever bought—there must be hundreds—can't just be lying about this house.'

'Not lying about the house, no,' agreed Mrs May.

'And all the other things we keep on buying. Again and again and again. Like pencils and match-boxes and sealing-wax and hair-slides and drawing-pins and thimbles—'

'And hat-pins,' put in Mrs May, 'and blotting-paper.'

'Yes, blotting-paper,' agreed Kate, 'but not hat-pins.'

'That's where you're wrong,' said Mrs May, and she picked up her work again. 'There was a reason for hat-pins.'

Kate stared. 'A reason?' she repeated. 'I mean—what kind of a reason?'

'Well, there were two reasons really. A hatpin is a very useful weapon and'—Mrs May laughed suddenly—'but it all sounds such nonsense and'—she hesitated—'it was so very long ago!'

'But tell me,' said Kate, 'tell me how you *know* about the hat-pin. Did you ever see one?'

Mrs May threw her a startled glance. 'Well, yes—,' she began.

'Not a hat-pin,' exclaimed Kate impatiently, 'a-whatever-you-called-them—a Borrower?'

Mrs May drew a sharp breath. 'No,' she said quickly, 'I never saw one.'

'But someone else saw one,' cried Kate, 'and you know about it. I can see you do!'

'Hush,' said Mrs May, 'no need to shout!' She gazed downwards at the upturned face and then she smiled and her eyes slid away into distance. 'I had a brother—' she began uncertainly.

Kate knelt upon the hassock. 'And he saw them!'

'I don't know,' said Mrs May, shaking her head, 'I just don't know!' She smoothed out her work upon her knee. 'He was such a tease. He told us so many things—my sister and me—impossible things. He was killed,' she added gently, 'many years ago now on the North-West Frontier. He became colonel of his regiment. He died what they call "a hero's death"…'

'Was he your only brother?'

'Yes, and he was our little brother. I think that was why'— she thought for a moment, still smiling to herself—'yes, why he told us such impossible stories, such strange imaginings. He was jealous, I think, because we were older and because

6

we could read better. He wanted to impress us; he wanted, perhaps, to shock us. And yet'—she looked into the fire—'there was something about him—perhaps because we were brought up in India among mystery and magic and legend—something that made us think that he saw things that other people could not see; sometimes we'd know he was teasing, but at other times—well, we were not so sure...' She leaned forward and, in her tidy way, brushed a fan of loose ashes under the grate, then, brush in hand, she stared again at the fire. 'He wasn't a very strong little boy: the first time he came home from India he got rheumatic fever. He missed a whole term at school and was sent away to the country to get over it. To the house of a great aunt. Later I went there myself. It was a strange old house...' She hung up the brush on its brass hook and, dusting her hands on her handkerchief, she picked up her work. 'Better light the lamp,' she said.

'Not yet,' begged Kate, leaning forward. 'Please go on. Please tell me—'

'But I've told you.'

'No you haven't. This old house—wasn't that where he saw—he saw...'

Mrs May laughed. 'Where he saw the Borrowers? Yes, that's what he told us... what he'd have us believe. And, what's more, it seems that he didn't just see them but that he got to know them very well; that he became part of their lives, as it were; in fact, you might almost say that he became a Borrower himself...'

'Oh,—tell me. Please. Try to remember. Right from the very beginning!'

'But I do remember,' said Mrs May. 'Oddly enough I remember it better than many real things which have happened. Perhaps it was a real thing. I just don't know. You see, on the way back to India my brother and I had to share a cabin—my sister used to sleep with our governess—and, on those very hot nights, often we couldn't sleep; and my brother would talk for hours and hours, going over old ground, repeating conversations, telling me details again and again—wondering how they were and what they were doing and—'

'They? Who were they—exactly?'

'Homily, Pod, and little Arrietty.'

'Pod?'

'Yes, even their names were never quite right. They imagined they had their own names quite different from human names—but with half an ear you could tell they were borrowed. Even Uncle Hendreary's and Eggletina's. Everything they had was borrowed; they had nothing of their own at all. Nothing. In spite of this, my brother said, they were touchy and conceited, and thought they owned the world.'

'How do you mean?'

'They thought human beings were just invented to do the dirty work—great slaves put there for them to use. At least, that's what they told each other. But my brother said that, underneath, he thought they were frightened. It was because they were frightened, he thought, that they had grown so small. Each generation had become smaller and smaller, and more and more hidden. In the olden days, it seems, and in some parts of England, our ancestors talked quite openly about the "little people".'

'Yes,' said Kate, 'I know.'

'Nowadays, I suppose,' Mrs May went on slowly, 'if they exist at all, you would only find them in houses which are old and quiet and deep in the country—and where the human beings live to a routine. Routine is their safeguard: it is important for them to know which rooms are to be used and when. They do not stay long where there are careless people, unruly children, or certain household pets.

'This particular old house, of course, was ideal—although as far as some of them were concerned, a trifle cold and empty. Great Aunt Sophy was bedridden, through a hunting accident some twenty years before, and as for other human beings there was only Mrs Driver the cook, Crampfurl the gardener, and, at rare intervals, an odd housemaid or such. My brother, too, when he went there after rheumatic fever, had to spend long hours in bed, and for those first weeks it seems the Borrowers did not know of his existence.

'He slept in the old night-nursery beyond the schoolroom. The schoolroom, at that time, was sheeted and shrouded and filled with junk—odd trunks, a broken sewing machine, a desk, a dressmaker's dummy, a table, some chairs, and a disused pianola—as the children who had used it, Great Aunt Sophy's children, had long since grown up, married, died, or gone away. The night-nursery opened out of the schoolroom and, from his bed, my brother could see the oil-painting of the battle of Waterloo which hung above the schoolroom fire-place and, on the wall, a corner cupboard with glass doors in which was set out, on hooks and shelves, a doll's tea-serv-ice—very delicate and old. At night, if the schoolroom door was open, he had a view down the lighted passage which led to the staircase, and it would comfort him to see, each evening at dusk, Mrs Driver appear at the head of the stairs and cross the passage carrying a tray for Aunt Sophy with Bath Oliver biscuits and the tall, cut-glass decanter of Fine Old Pale Madeira. On her way out Mrs Driver would pause and lower the gas jet in the passage to a dim, blue flame, and then he would watch her as she stumped away downstairs, sinking slowly out of sight between the banisters.

'Under this passage, in the hall below, there was a clock, and through the night he would hear it strike the hours. It was a grandfather clock and very old. Mr Frith of Leighton Buzzard came each month to wind it, as his father had come before him and his great-uncle before that. For eighty years, they said (and to Mr Frith's certain knowledge), it had not stopped and, as far as anyone could tell, for as many years before that. The great thing was that it must never be moved. It stood against the wain-scot, and the stone flags around it had been washed so often that a little platform, my brother said, rose up inside.

'And, under this clock, below the wainscot, there was a hole...'

CHAPTER TWO

It was Pod's hole—the keep of his fortress; the entrance to his home. Not that his home was anywhere near the clock: far from it—as you might say. There were yards of dark and dusty passage-way, with wooden doors between the joists and metal gates against the mice. Pod used all kinds of things for these gates—a flat leaf of a folding cheesegrater, the hinged lid of a small cash-box, squares of pierced zinc from an old meat-safe, a wire fly swotter... 'Not that I'm afraid of mice,' Homily would say, 'but I can't abide the smell.' In vain Arrietty had begged for a little mouse of her own, a little blind mouse to bring up by hand—'like Eggletina had had'. But Homily would bang with the pan lids and exclaim: 'And look what happened to Eggletina!' 'What,' Arrietty would ask, 'what did happen to Eggletina?' But no one would ever say.

It was only Pod who knew the way through the intersecting passages to the hole under the clock. And only Pod could open the gates. There were complicated clasps made of hairslides and safety-pins of which Pod alone knew the secret. His wife and child led more sheltered lives in homelike apartments under the kitchen, far removed from the risks and dangers of the dreaded house above. But there was a grating in the brick wall of the house, just below the floor level of the kitchen above, through which Arrietty could see the garden—a piece of gravelled path and a bank where crocuses bloomed in spring; where blossom drifted from an unseen tree; and where later an azalea bush would flower; and where birds came—and pecked and flirted and sometimes fought. 'The hours you waste on them birds,' Homily would say, 'and when there's a little job to be done you can never find the time. I was brought up in a house,' Homily went on, 'where there wasn't no grating, and we were all the happier for it. Now go off and get me the potato.'

That was the day when Arrietty, rolling the potato before her from the storehouse down the dusty lane under the floorboards, kicked it ill-temperedly so that it rolled rather fast into their kitchen, where Homily was stooping over the stove.

'There you go again,' exclaimed Homily, turning angrily; 'nearly pushed me into the soup. And when I say "potato" I don't mean the whole potato. Take the scissor, can't you, and cut off a slice.'

'Didn't know how much you wanted,' Arrietty had mumbled, as Homily, snorting and sniffing, unhooked the blade and handle of half a pair of manicure scissors from a nail on the wall, and began to cut through the peel.

'You've ruined this potato,' she grumbled. 'You can't roll it back now in all that dust, not once it's been cut open.'

'Oh, what does it matter?' said Arrietty. 'There are plenty more.'

'That's a nice way to talk. Plenty more. Do you realize,' Homily went on gravely, laying down the half nail scissor, 'that your poor father risks his life every time he borrows a potato?'

'I meant,' said Arrietty, 'that there are plenty more in the store-room.'

'Well, out of my way now,' said Homily, bustling around again, 'whatever you meant and let me get the supper.'

Arrietty had wandered through the open door into the sitting-room—the fire had been lighted and the room looked bright and cosy. Homily was proud of her sitting-room: the walls had been papered with scraps of old letters out of waste-paper baskets, and Homily had arranged the handwriting sideways in vertical stripes which ran from floor to ceiling. On the walls, repeated in various colours, hung several portraits of Queen Victoria as a girl; these were postage stamps, borrowed by Pod some years ago from the stamp-box on the desk in the morning-room. There was a lacquer trinket-box, padded inside and with the lid open, which they used as a settle; and that useful stand-by—a chest of drawers made of match-boxes. There was a round table with a red velvet cloth, which Pod had made from the wooden bottom of a pill-box supported on the carved pedestal of a knight from the chess-set. (This had caused a great deal of trouble upstairs when Aunt Sophy's eldest son, on a flying midweek visit, had invited the vicar for 'a game after dinner'. Rosa Pickhatchet, who was housemaid at the time, gave in her notice. Not long after she had left other things were found to be missing and, from that time onwards, Mrs Driver ruled supreme.) The knight itself—its bust, so to speak—was standing on a column in the corner, where it looked very fine, and lent that air to the room which only statuary can give.

Beside the fire, in a tilted wooden book-case, stood Arrietty's library. This was a set of those miniature volumes which the Victorians loved to print, but which to Arrietty seemed the size of very large church Bibles. There was Bryce's *Tom Thumb Gazetteer of the World*, including the last census; Bryce's *Tom Thumb Dictionary,* with short explanations of scientific, philosophical, literary, and technical terms; Bryce's *Tom Thumb Edition of the Comedies of William Shakespeare*, including a foreword on the author; another book, whose pages were all blank, called *Memoranda*; and, last but not least, Arrietty's favourite, Bryce's *Tom Thumb Diary and Proverb Book* with a saying for each day of the year and, as a preface, the life story of a little man called General Tom Thumb, who married a girl called Mercy Lavinia Bump. There was an engraving of their carriage and pair, with little horses—the size of mice. Arrietty was not a stupid girl. She knew that horses could not be as small as mice, but she did not realize that Tom Thumb, nearly two feet high, would seem a giant to a Borrower.

Arrietty had learned to read from these books, and to write by leaning sideways and copying out the writings on the walls. In spite of this, she did not always keep her diary, although on most days she would take the book out for the sake of the saying, which sometimes would comfort her. Today it said: 'You may go farther and fare worse' and, underneath: 'Order of the Garter, instituted 1348.' She carried the book to the fire and sat down with her feet on the hob.

'What are you doing, Arrietty?' called Homily from the kitchen.

'Writing my diary.'

'Oh,' exclaimed Homily shortly.

'What did you want?' asked Arrietty. She felt quite safe; Homily liked her to write; Homily encouraged any form of culture. Homily herself, poor ignorant creature, could not even say the alphabet. 'Nothing. Nothing,' said Homily crossly, banging away with the pan lids; 'it'll do later.'

Arrietty took out her pencil. It was a small white pencil, with a piece of silk cord attached, which had come off a dance programme, but, even so, in Arrietty's hand, it looked like a rolling-pin.

'Arrietty!' called Homily again from the kitchen.

'Yes?'

'Put a little something on the fire, will you?'

Arrietty braced her muscles and heaved the book off her knees, and stood it upright on the floor. They kept the fuel, assorted slack and crumbled candle grease, in a pewter mustard-pot, and shovelled it out with the spoon. Arrietty trickled only a few grains, tilting the mustard spoon, not to spoil the blaze. Then she stood there basking in the warmth. It was a charming fire-place, made by Arrietty's grandfather, with a cog wheel from the stables, part of an old cider-press. The spokes of the cog-wheel stood out in starry rays, and the fire itself nestled in the centre. Above there was a chimney-piece made from a small brass funnel, inverted. This, at one time, belonged to an oil-lamp which matched it, and which stood, in the old days, on the hall table upstairs. An arrangement of pipes, from the spout of the funnel, carried the fumes into the kitchen flues above. The fire was laid with match-sticks and fed with assorted slack and, as it burned up, the iron would become hot, and Homily would simmer soup on the spokes, in a silver thimble, and Arrietty would broil nuts. How cosy those winter evenings could be. Arrietty, her great book on her knees, sometimes reading aloud; Pod at his last (he was a shoemaker, and made button-boots out of kid-gloves—now, alas, only for his family); and Homily, quiet at last, with her knitting.

Homily knitted their jerseys and stockings on black head-ed pins, and, sometimes, on darning needles. A great reel of silk or cotton would stand, table high, beside her chair, and sometimes, if she pulled too sharply, the reel would tip up and roll away out of the open door into the dusty passage beyond, and Arrietty would be sent after it, to rewind it care-fully as she rolled it back.

The floor of the sitting-room was carpeted with deep red blotting-paper, which was warm and cosy, and soaked up the spills. Homily would renew it at intervals when it became available upstairs, but since Aunt Sophy had taken to her bed, Mrs Driver seldom thought of blotting-paper unless, suddenly, there were guests. Homily liked things which saved washing because drying was difficult under the floor; water they had in plenty, hot and cold, thanks to Pod's father, who had tapped the pipes from the kitchen boiler. They bathed in a small tureen, which once had held *pâté de foie gras*. When you had wiped out your bath you were supposed to put the lid back, to stop people putting things in it. The soap, too, a great cake of it, hung on a nail in the scullery, and they scraped pieces off. Homily liked coal tar, but Pod and Arrietty preferred sandalwood.

'What are you doing now, Arrietty?' called Homily from the kitchen.

'Still writing my diary.'

Once again Arrietty took hold of the book and heaved it back on to her knees. She licked the lead of her great pencil, and stared a moment, deep in thought. She allowed herself (when she did remember to write) one little line on each page because she would never—of this she was sure—have another diary, and if she could get twenty lines on each page the diary would last her twenty years. She had kept it for nearly two years already, and today, 22 March, she read last year's entry: 'Mother cross.' She thought a while longer then, at last, she put ditto marks under 'Mother', and 'worried' under 'cross'.

'What did you say you were doing, Arrietty?' called Homily from the kitchen.

Arrietty closed the book. 'Nothing,' she said.

'Then chop me up this onion, there's a good girl. Your father's late tonight...'

CHAPTER THREE

Sighing, Arrietty put away her diary and went into the kitchen. She took the onion ring from Homily and slung it lightly round her shoulders, while she foraged for a piece of razor blade. 'Really, Arrietty,' exclaimed Homily, 'not on your clean jersey! Do you want to smell like a bit-bucket? Here, take the scissor—'

Arrietty stepped through the onion ring as though it were a child's hoop, and began to chop it into segments.

'Your father's late,' muttered Homily again, 'and it's my fault, as you might say. Oh dear, oh dear, I wish I hadn't—'

'Hadn't what?' asked Arrietty, her eyes watering. She sniffed loudly and longed to rub her nose on her sleeve.

Homily pushed back a thin lock of hair with a worried hand. She stared at Arrietty absently. 'It's that tea-cup you broke,' she said.

'But that was days ago—' began Arrietty, blinking her eyelids, and she sniffed again.

'I know. I know. It's not you. It's me. It's not the breaking that matters, it's what I said to your father.'

'What did you say to him?'

'Well, I just said—there's the rest of the service, I said—up there, where it always was, in the corner cupboard in the schoolroom.'

'I don't see anything bad in that,' said Arrietty as, one by one, she dropped the pieces of onion into the soup.

'But it's a high cupboard,' exclaimed Homily. 'You have to get up by the curtain. And your father at his age—' She sat down suddenly on a metal-topped champagne cork. 'Oh, Arrietty I wish I'd never mentioned it!'

'Don't worry,' said Arrietty, 'papa knows what he can do.' She pulled a rubber scent-bottle cork out of the hole in the hot water pipe and let a trickle of scalding drops fall into the tin lid of an aspirin bottle. She added cold and began to wash her hands.

'Maybe,' said Homily. 'But I went on about it so. What's a tea-cup! Your Uncle Hendreary never drank a thing that wasn't out of a common acorn cup, and he's lived to a ripe old age and had the strength to emigrate. My mother's family never had nothing but a little bone thimble which they shared around. But it's once you've *had* a tea-cup, if you see what I mean…'

'Yes,' said Arrietty, drying her hands on a roller towel made out of surgical bandage.

'It's that curtain,' cried Homily. 'He can't climb a curtain at his age—not by the bobbles!'

'With his pin he could,' said Arrietty.

'His pin! I led him into that one too! Take a hat-pin, I told him, and tie a bit of name-tape to the head, and pull yourself upstairs. It was to borrow the emerald watch from Her bedroom for me to time the cooking.' Homily's voice began to tremble. 'Your mother's a wicked woman, Arrietty. Wicked and selfish, that's what she is!'

'You know what?' exclaimed Arrietty suddenly.

Homily brushed away a tear 'No,' she said wanly, 'what?'

'I could climb a curtain.'

Homily rose up. 'Arrietty you dare stand there in cold blood and say a thing like that!'

'But I could! I could! I could borrow! I know I could!'

'Oh!' gasped Homily. 'Oh, you wicked heathen girl! How could you speak so!' and she crumpled up again on the cork stool. 'So it's come to this!' she said.

'Now, mother, please,' begged Arrietty, 'now, don't take on!'

'But don't you see, Arrietty...' gasped Homily; she stared down at the table at a loss for words and then, at last, she raised a haggard face. 'My poor child,' she said, 'don't speak like that of borrowing. You don't know—and, thank goodness, you never will know'—she dropped her voice to a fearful whisper—'what it's like upstairs...'

Arrietty was silent. 'What is it like?' she asked after a moment.

Homily wiped her face on her apron and smoothed back her hair. 'Your Uncle Hendreary,' she began, 'Eggletina's father,' and then she paused. 'Listen!' she said. 'What's that?'

Echoing on the wood was a faint vibration—the sound of

a distant click. 'Your father!' exclaimed Homily. 'Oh, look at me! Where's the comb?'

They had a comb: a little, silver, eighteenth-century eye-brow comb from the cabinet in the drawing-room upstairs. Homily ran it through her hair and rinsed her poor red eyes and, when Pod came in, she was smiling and smoothing down her apron.

CHAPTER FOUR

Pod came in slowly, his sack on his back; he leaned his hat-pin, with its dangling name-tape, against the wall and, on the middle of the kitchen table, he placed a doll's tea-cup; it seemed the size of a mixing-bowl.

'Why, Pod—' began Homily.

'Got the saucer too,' he said. He swung down the sack and untied the neck. 'Here you are,' he said, drawing out the saucer. 'Matches it.'

He had a round, currant-bunny sort of face; tonight it looked flabby.

'Oh, Pod,' said Homily, 'you do look queer. Are you all right?'

Pod sat down. 'I'm fair enough,' he said.

'You went up the curtain,' said Homily. 'Oh, Pod, you shouldn't have. It's shaken you—'

Pod made a strange face, his eyes swivelled round towards Arrietty. Homily stared at him, her mouth open, and then she turned. 'Come along, Arrietty,' she said briskly, 'you pop off to bed, now, like a good girl, and I'll bring you some supper.'

'Oh,' said Arrietty, 'can't I see the rest of the borrowings?'

'Your father's got nothing now. Only food. Off you pop to bed. You've seen the cup and saucer.'

Arrietty went into the sitting-room to put away her diary, and took some time fixing her candle on the upturned drawing-pin which served as a holder.

'Whatever are you doing?' grumbled Homily. 'Give it here. There, that's the way. Now off to bed and fold your clothes, mind.'

'Good night, papa,' said Arrietty kissing his flat white cheek.

'Careful of the light,' he said mechanically, and watched her with his round eyes until she had closed the door.

'Now, Pod,' said Homily, when they were alone, 'tell me. What's the matter?'

Pod looked at her blankly. 'I been "seen",' he said.

Homily put out a groping hand for the edge of the table; she grasped it and lowered herself slowly on to the stool. 'Oh, Pod,' she said.

There was silence between them. Pod stared at Homily and Homily stared at the table. After a while she raised her white face. 'Badly?' she asked.

Pod moved restlessly. 'I don't know about badly. I been "seen". Ain't that bad enough?'

'No one,' said Homily slowly, 'hasn't never been "seen" since Uncle Hendreary and he was the first they say for forty-five years.' A thought struck her and she gripped the table. 'It's no good, Pod, I won't emigrate!'

'No one's asked you to,' said Pod.

'To go and live like Hendreary and Lupy in a badger's set!

The other side of the world, that's where they say it is—all among the earthworms.'

'It's two fields away, above the spinney,' said Pod.

'Nuts, that's what they eat. And berries. I wouldn't wonder if they don't eat mice—'

'You've eaten mice yourself,' Pod reminded her.

'All draughts and fresh air and the children growing up wild. Think of Arrietty!' said Homily. 'Think of the way she's been brought up. An only child. She'd catch her death. It's different for Hendreary.'

'Why?' asked Pod. 'He's got five.'

'That's why,' explained Homily. 'When you've got five, they're brought up rough. But never mind that now... Who saw you?'

'A boy,' said Pod.

'A what?' exclaimed Homily, staring.

'A boy.' Pod sketched out a rough shape in the air with his hands. 'You know, a boy.'

'But there isn't—I mean, what sort of a boy?'

'I don't know what you mean "what sort of a boy". A boy in a night-shirt. A boy. You know what a boy is, don't you?'

'Yes,' said Homily, 'I know what a boy is. But there hasn't been a boy, not in this house, these twenty years.'

'Well,' said Pod, 'there's one here now.'

Homily stared at him in silence, and Pod met her eyes. 'Where did he see you?' asked Homily at last.

'In the schoolroom.'

'Oh,' said Homily, 'when you was getting the cup?'

'Yes,' said Pod.

'Haven't you got eyes?' asked Homily. 'Couldn't you have looked first?'

'There's never nobody in the schoolroom. And what's more,' he went on, 'there wasn't today.'

'Then where was he?'

'In bed. In the night-nursery or whatever it's called. That's where he was. Sitting up in bed. With the doors open.'

'Well, you could have looked in the nursery.'

'How could I—half-way up the curtain!'

'Is that where you was?'

'Yes.'

'With the cup?'

'Yes. I couldn't get up or down.'

'Oh, Pod,' wailed Homily, 'I should never have let you go. Not at your age!'

'Now, look here,' said Pod, 'don't mistake me. I got up all right. Got up like a bird, as you might say, bobbles or no bobbles. But'—he leaned towards her—'afterwards—with the cup in me hand, if you see what I mean...' He picked it up off the table. 'You see, it's heavy like. You can hold it by the handle, like this but it drops or droops, as you might say. You should take a cup like this in your two hands. A bit of cheese off a shelf, or an apple—well, I drop that... give it a push and it falls and I climbs down in me own time and picks it up. But with a cup—you see what I mean? And coming down, you got to watch your feet. And, as I say, some of the bobbles was missing. You didn't know what you could hold on to, not safely…'

'Oh, Pod,' said Homily, her eyes full of tears, 'what did you do?'

'Well,' said Pod, sitting back again, 'he took the cup.'

'What do you mean?' exclaimed Homily, aghast.

Pod avoided her eyes. 'Well, he'd been sitting up in bed there watching me. I'd been on that curtain a good ten minutes, because the hall clock had just struck the quarter—'

'But how do you mean—"he took the cup"?'

'Well, he'd got out of bed and there he was standing, looking up. "I'll take the cup," he said.'

'Oh!' gasped Homily, her eyes staring. 'And you give it to him?'

'He took it,' said Pod, 'ever so gentle. And then, when I was down, he give it me.' Homily put her face in her hands. 'Now don't take on,' said Pod uneasily.

'He might have caught you,' shuddered Homily in a stifled voice.

'Yes,' said Pod, 'but he just give me the cup. "Here you are," he said.'

Homily raised her face. 'What are we going to do?' she asked.

Pod sighed. 'Well, there isn't nothing we can do. Except—'

'Oh, no,' exclaimed Homily, 'not that. Not emigrate. Not that, Pod, now I've got the house so nice and a clock and all.'

'We could take the clock,' said Pod.

'And Arrietty? What about her? She's not like those cousins. She can *read*, Pod, and sew a treat—'

'He don't know where we live,' said Pod.

'But they look,' exclaimed Homily. 'Remember Hendreary! They got the cat and—'

'Now, now,' said Pod, 'don't bring up the past.'

'But you've got to think of it! They got the cat and—'

'Yes,' said Pod, 'but Eggletina was different.'

'How different? She was Arrietty's age.'

'Well, they hadn't told her, you see. That's where they went wrong. They tried to make her believe that there wasn't nothing but was under the floor. They never told her about Mrs Driver or Crampfurl. Least of all about cats.'

'There wasn't any cat,' Homily pointed out, 'not till Hendreary was "seen".'

'Well, there was, then,' said Pod. 'You got to tell them, that's what I say, or they try to find out for themselves.'

'Pod,' said Homily solemnly, 'we haven't told Arrietty.'

'Oh, she knows,' said Pod; he moved uncomfortably. 'She's got her grating.'

'She doesn't know about Eggletina. She doesn't know about being "seen".'

'Well,' said Pod, 'we'll tell her. We always said we would. There's no hurry.'

Homily stood up. 'Pod,' she said, 'we're going to tell her tonight.'

CHAPTER FIVE

Arrietty had not been asleep. She had been lying under her knotted coverlet staring up at the ceiling. It was an interesting ceiling. Pod had built Arrietty's bedroom out of two cigar-boxes, and on the ceiling lovely painted ladies dressed in swirls of chiffon blew long trumpets against a background of blue sky; below there were feathery palm-trees and small white houses set about a square. It was a glamorous scene, above all by candlelight, but tonight Arrietty had stared without seeing. The wood of a cigar-box is thin and Arrietty, lying straight and still under the quilt, had heard the rise and fall of worried voices. She had heard her own name; she had heard Homily exclaim: 'Nuts and berries, that's what they eat!' and she had heard, after a while, the heart-felt cry of 'What shall we do?'

So when Homily appeared beside her bed, she wrapped herself obediently in her quilt and, padding in her bare feet along the dusty passage, she joined her parents in the warmth of the kitchen. Crouched on her little stool, she sat clasping her knees, shivering a little, and looking from one face to another.

Homily came beside her and, kneeling on the floor, she placed an arm round Arrietty's skinny shoulders. 'Arrietty,' she said gravely, 'you know about upstairs?'

'What about it?' asked Arrietty.

'You know about the two giants?'

'Yes,' said Arrietty, 'Great Aunt Sophy and Mrs Driver.'

'That's right,' said Homily, 'and Crampfurl in the garden.' She laid a roughened hand on Arrietty's clasped ones. 'You know about Uncle Hendreary?'

Arrietty thought awhile. 'He went abroad?' she said.

'Emigrated,' corrected Homily, 'to the other side of the world. With Aunt Lupy and all the children. To a badger's set—a hole in a bank under a hawthorn hedge. Now why do you think he did this?'

'Oh,' said Arrietty, her face alight, 'to be out of doors... to lie in the sun... to run in the grass... to swing on twigs like the birds do... to suck honey...'

'Nonsense, Arrietty,' exclaimed Homily sharply, 'that's a nasty habit! And your Uncle Hendreary's a rheumatic sort of man. He emigrated,' she went on, stressing the word, 'because he was "seen".'

'Oh,' said Arrietty.

'He was "seen" on 23rd of April, 1892, by Rosa Pickhatchet, on the drawing-room mantelpiece. Of all places...' she added suddenly in a wondering aside.

'Oh,' said Arrietty.

'I have never heard nor no one has never seen fit to tell why he went on the drawing-room mantelpiece in the first place. There's nothing on it, your father assures me, which cannot be seen from the floor or by standing sideways on the handle of the bureau and steadying yourself on the key. That's what your father does if he ever goes into the drawing-room—'

'They said it was a liver pill,' put in Pod.

'How do you mean?' asked Homily, startled.

'A liver pill for Lupy' Pod spoke wearily. 'Someone started a rumour,' he went on, that there were liver pills on the drawing-room mantelpiece…'

'Oh,' said Homily and looked thoughtful, 'I never heard that. All the same,' she exclaimed, 'it was stupid and foolhardy. There's no way down except by the bell-pull. She dusted him, they say, with a feather duster, and he stood so still, alongside a cupid, that she might never have noticed him if he hadn't sneezed. She was new, you see, and didn't know the ornaments. We heard her screeching right here under the kitchen. And they could never get her to clean anything much after that that wasn't chairs or tables—least of all the tiger-skin rug.'

'I don't hardly never bother with the drawing-room,' said Pod. 'Everything's got its place like and they see what goes. There might be a little something left on a table or down the side of a chair, but not without there's been company, and there never is no company—not for the last ten or twelve year. Sitting here in this chair, I can tell you by heart every blessed thing that's in that drawing-room, working round from the cabinet by the window to the—'

'There's a mint of things in that cabinet,' interrupted Homily, 'solid silver some of them. A solid-silver violin, they got there, strings and all—just right for our Arrietty.'

'What's the good,' asked Pod, 'of things behind glass?'

'Couldn't you break it?' suggested Arrietty. 'Just a corner, just a little tap, just a...' Her voice faltered as she saw the shocked amazement on her father's face.

'Listen here, Arrietty,' began Homily angrily, and then she controlled herself and patted Arrietty's clasped hands. 'She don't know much about borrowing,' she explained to Pod. 'You can't blame her.' She turned again to Arrietty. 'Borrowing's a skilled job, an art like. Of all the families who've been in this house, there's only us left, and do you know for why? Because your father, Arrietty, is the best Borrower that's been known in these parts since—well, before your grandad's time. Even your Aunt Lupy admitted that much. When he was younger I've seen your father walk the length of a laid dinner-table, after the gong was rung, taking a nut or sweet from every dish, and down by a fold in the tablecloth as the first people came in at the door. He'd do it just for fun, wouldn't you, Pod?'

Pod smiled wanly. 'There weren't no sense in it,' he said.

'Maybe,' said Homily, 'but you did it! Who else would dare?'

'I were younger then,' said Pod. He sighed and turned to Arrietty. 'You don't break things, lass. That's not the way to do it. That's not borrowing... '

'We were rich then,' said Homily 'Oh, we did have some lovely things! You were only a tot, Arrietty, and wouldn't remember. We had a whole suite of walnut furniture out of the doll's house and a set of wineglasses in green glass, and a musical snuff-box, and the cousins would come and we'd have parties. Do you remember, Pod? Not only the cousins. The Harpsichords came. Everybody came—except those Overmantels from the morning-room. And we'd dance and dance and the young people would sit out by the grating. Three tunes that snuff-box played—*Clementine, God Save the Queen*, and the *Post Chaise Gallop*. We were the envy of everybody—even the Overmantels…'

'Who were the Overmantels?' asked Arrietty.

'Oh, you must've heard me talk of the Overmantels,' exclaimed Homily, 'that stuck-up lot who lived in the wall high up—among the lath and plaster behind the mantelpiece in the morning-room. And a queer lot they were. The men smoked all the time because the tobacco jars were kept there; and they'd climb about and in and out the carvings of the overmantel, sliding down pillars and showing off. The women were a conceited lot too, always admiring themselves in all those bits of overmantel looking-glass. They never asked anyone up there and I, for one, never wanted to go. I've no head for heights, and your father never liked the men. He's always lived steady, your father has, and not only the tobacco jars, but the whisky decanters too, were kept in the morning-room and they say those Overmantel men would suck up the dregs in the glasses through those quill pipe-cleaners they keep there on the mantelpiece. I don't know whether it's true but they do say that those Overmantel men used to have a party every Tuesday after the bailiff had been to talk business in the morning-room. Laid out, they'd be, dead drunk—or so the story goes—on the green plush tablecloth, all among the tin boxes and the account books—'

'Now, Homily,' protested Pod, who did not like gossip, 'I never see'd 'em.'

'But you wouldn't put it past them, Pod. You said yourself when I married you not to call on the Overmantels.'

'They lived so high,' said Pod, 'that's all.'

'Well, they were a lazy lot—that much you can't deny. They never had no kind of home life. Kept themselves warm in winter by the heat of the morning-room fire and ate nothing but breakfast food; breakfast, of course, was the only meal served in the morning-room.'

'What happened to them?' asked Arrietty.

'Well, when the Master died and She took to her bed, there was no more use for the morning-room. So the Overmantels had to go. What else could they do? No food, no fire. It's a bitter cold room in winter.'

'And the Harpsichords?' asked Arrietty.

Homily looked thoughtful. 'Well, they were different. I'm not saying they weren't stuck up too, because they were. Your Aunt Lupy, who married your Uncle Hendreary, was a Harpsichord by marriage and we all know the airs she gave herself.'

'Now, Homily—' began Pod.

'Well, she'd no right to. She was only a Rain-Pipe from the stables before she married Harpsichord.'

'Didn't she marry Uncle Hendreary?' asked Arrietty.

'Yes, later. She was a widow with two children and he was a widower with three. It's no good looking at me like that, Pod. You can't deny she took it out of poor Hendreary: she thought it was a comedown to marry a Clock.'

'Why?' asked Arrietty.

'Because we Clocks live under the kitchen, that's why. Because we don't talk fancy grammar and eat anchovy toast. But to live under the kitchen doesn't say we aren't educated. The Clocks are just as old a family as the Harpsichords. You remember that, Arrietty, and don't let anyone tell you different. Your grandfather could count and write down the numbers up to—what was it, Pod?'

'Fifty-seven,' said Pod.

'There,' said Homily, 'fifty-seven! And your father can count, as you know, Arrietty; he can count and write down the numbers, on and on, as far as it goes. How far does it go, Pod?'

'Close on a thousand,' said Pod.

'There!' exclaimed Homily. 'And he knows the alphabet because he taught you, Arrietty, didn't he? And he would have been able to read—wouldn't you, Pod?—if he hadn't had to start borrowing so young. Your Uncle Hendreary and your father had to go out borrowing at thirteen—your age,

Arrietty, think of it!'

'But I should like——' began Arrietty.

'So he didn't have your advantages,' went on Homily breathlessly, 'and just because the Harpsichords lived in the drawing-room—they moved in there, in 1837, to a hole in the wainscot just behind where the harpsichord used to stand, if ever there was one, which I doubt—and were really a family called Linen-Press or some such name and changed it to Harpsichord——'

'What did they live on,' asked Arrietty, 'in the drawing-room?'

'Afternoon tea,' said Homily, 'nothing but afternoon tea. No wonder the children grew up peaky. Of course, in the old days it was better muffins and crumpets and such, and good rich cake and jams and jellies. And there was one old Harpsichord who could remember syllabub of an evening. But they had to do their borrowing in such a rush, poor things. On wet days, when the human beings sat all afternoon in the drawing-room, the tea would be brought in and taken away again without a chance of the Harpsichords getting near it—and on fine days it might be taken out into the garden. Lupy has told me that, sometimes, there were days and days when they lived on crumbs and on water out of the flower-vases. So you can't be too hard on them; their only comfort, poor things, was to show off a bit and talk like ladies and gentlemen. Did you ever hear your Aunt Lupy talk?'

'Yes. No. I can't remember.'

'Oh, you should have heard her say "Parquet"—that's the stuff the drawing-room floor's made of—"Parkay... Parr-r-kay", she'd say. Oh, it was lovely. Come to think of it, your Aunt Lupy was the most stuck up of them all...'

'Arrietty's shivering,' said Pod. 'We didn't get the little maid up to talk about Aunt Lupy.'

'Nor we did,' cried Homily, suddenly contrite, 'you should've stopped me, Pod. There, my lamb, tuck this quilt right round you and I'll get you a nice drop of piping hot soup!'

'And yet,' said Pod as Homily, fussing at the stove, ladled soup into the tea-cup, 'we did in a way.'

'Did what?' asked Homily.

'Get her up to talk about Aunt Lupy. Aunt Lupy Uncle Hendreary, and'—he paused 'Eggletina.'

'Let her drink up her soup first,' said Homily.

'There's no call for her to stop drinking,' said Pod.

CHAPTER SIX

Your mother and I got you up,' said Pod, 'to tell you about upstairs.'

Arrietty, holding the great cup in both hands, looked at him over the edge.

Pod coughed. 'You said a while back that the sky was dark brown with cracks in it. Well, it isn't.' He looked at her almost accusingly. 'It's blue.'

'I know,' said Arrietty.

'You know!' exclaimed Pod.

'Yes, of course I know. I've got the grating.'

'Can you see the sky through the grating?'

'Go on,' interrupted Homily, 'tell her about the gates.'

'Well,' said Pod ponderously, 'if you go outside this room, what do you see?'

'A dark passage,' said Arrietty.

'And what else?'

'Other rooms.'

'And if you go farther?'

'More passages.'

'And, if you go walking on and on, in all the passages under the floor, however they twist and turn, what do you find?'

'Gates,' said Arrietty.

'Strong gates,' said Pod, 'gates you can't open. What are they there for?'

'Against the mice?' said Arrietty.

'Yes,' agreed Pod uncertainly, as though he gave her half a mark, 'but mice never hurt no one. What else?'

'Rats?' suggested Arrietty.

'We don't have rats,' said Pod. 'What about cats?'

'Cats?' echoed Arrietty surprised.

'Or to keep you in?' suggested Pod.

'To keep me in?' repeated Arrietty dismayed.

'Upstairs is a dangerous place,' said Pod. 'And you, Arrietty you're all we've got, see? It isn't like Hendreary—he still has two of his own and two of hers. Once,' said Pod, 'Hendreary had three—three of his own.'

'Your father's thinking of Eggletina,' said Homily.

'Yes,' said Pod, 'Eggletina. They never told her about upstairs. And they hadn't got no grating. They told her the sky was nailed up, like, with cracks in it—'

'A foolish way to bring up a child,' murmured Homily. She sniffed slightly and touched Arrietty's hair.

'But Eggletina was no fool,' said Pod; 'she didn't believe them. So one day,' he went on, 'she went upstairs to see for herself.'

'How did she get out?' asked Arrietty, interested.

'Well, we didn't have so many gates then. Just the one under the clock. Hendreary must have left it unlocked or something. Anyway, Eggletina went out...'

'In a blue dress,' said Homily, 'and a pair of button-boots your father made her, yellow kid with jet beads for buttons. Lovely they were.'

'Well,' said Pod, 'any other time it might have been all right. She'd have gone out, had a look around, had a bit of a fright, maybe, and come back—none the worse and no one the wiser...'

'But things had been happening,' said Homily.

'Yes,' said Pod, 'she didn't know, as they never told her, that her father had been "seen" and that upstairs they had got in the cat and—'

'They waited a week,' said Homily, 'and they waited a month and they hoped for a year but no one ever saw Eggletina no more.'

'And that,' said Pod after a pause and eyeing Arrietty, 'is what happened to Eggletina.'

There was silence except for Pod's breathing and the faint bubble of the soup.

'It just broke up your Uncle Hendreary,' said Homily at last. 'He never went upstairs again in case, he said, he found the button-boots. Their only future was to emigrate.'

Arrietty was silent a moment, then she raised her head. 'Why did you tell me?' she asked. 'Now? Tonight?'

Homily got up. She moved restlessly towards the stove. 'We don't never talk of it,' she said, 'at least, not much, but tonight, we felt—' She turned suddenly. 'Well, we'll just say it straight out: your father's been "seen", Arrietty!'

'Oh,' said Arrietty, 'who by?'

'Well, by a—something you've never heard of. But that's not the point: the point is—'

'You think they'll get a cat?'

'They may,' said Homily.

Arrietty set down the soup for a moment; she stared into the cup as it stood beside her almost knee high on the floor; there was a dreamy, secret something about her lowered face. 'Couldn't we emigrate?' she ventured at last, very softly.

Homily gasped and clasped her hands and swung away towards the wall. 'You don't know what you're talking about,' she cried, addressing a frying-pan which hung there. 'Worms and weasels and cold and damp and—'

'But supposing,' said Arrietty, 'that I went out, like Eggletina did, and the cat ate *me*. Then you and papa would emigrate. Wouldn't you?' she asked, and her voice faltered. 'Wouldn't you?'

Homily swung round again, this time towards Arrietty; her face looked very angry. 'I shall smack you, Arrietty Clock, if you don't behave yourself this minute!'

Arrietty's eyes filled with tears. 'I was only thinking,' she said, 'that I'd like to be there—to emigrate too. Uneaten,' she added softly and the tears fell.

'Now,' said Pod, 'this is enough! You get off to bed, Arrietty, uneaten and unbeaten both and we'll talk about it in the morning.'

'It's not that I'm afraid,' cried Arrietty angrily; 'I like cats. I bet the cat didn't eat Eggletina. I bet she just ran away because she hated being cooped up... day after day week after week... year after year... Like I do!' she added on a sob.

'Cooped up!' repeated Homily, astounded.

Arrietty put her face into her hands. 'Gates...' she gasped, 'gates, gates, gates...'

Pod and Homily stared at each other across Arrietty's bowed shoulders. 'You didn't ought to have brought it up,' he said unhappily, 'not so late at night...'

Arrietty raised her tear-streaked face. 'Late or early, what's the difference?' she cried. 'Oh, I know papa is a wonderful Borrower. I know we've managed to stay when all the others have gone. But what has it done for us, in the end? I don't think it's so clever to live on alone, for ever and ever, in a great, big, half-empty house; under the floor, with no one to talk to, no one to play with, nothing to see but dust and passages, no light but candlelight and firelight and what comes through the cracks. Eggletina had brothers and Eggletina had half-brothers; Eggletina had a tame mouse; Eggletina had yellow boots with jet buttons, and Eggletina did get out—just once!'

'Shush,' said Pod gently, 'not so loud.' Above their heads the floor creaked and heavy footfalls heaved deliberately to and fro. They heard Mrs Driver's grumbling voice and the clatter of the fireirons. 'Drat this stove,' they heard her say, 'wind's in the east again.' Then they heard her raise her voice and call, 'Crampfurl!'

Pod sat staring glumly at the floor; Arrietty shivered a little and hugged herself more lightly into the knitted quilt and
Homily drew a long, slow breath. Suddenly she raised her
head.

'The child is right,' she announced firmly.

Arrietty's eyes grew big. 'Oh, no—' she began. It shocked
her to be right. Parents were right, not children. Children
could say anything, Arrietty knew, and enjoy saying it know-
ing always they were safe and wrong.

'You see, Pod,' went on Homily, 'it was different for you
and me. There was other families, other children... the Sinks
in the scullery, you remember? And those people who lived
behind the knife machine—I forget their names now. And the
Broom Cupboard boys. And there was that underground passage from the stables—you know, that the Rain-Pipes used.
We had more, as you might say, freedom.'

'Ah, yes,' said Pod, 'in a way. But where does freedom
take you?' He looked up uncertainly. 'Where are they all
now?'

'Some of them may have bettered themselves, I shouldn't
wonder,' said Homily sharply. 'Times have changed in the
whole house. Pickings aren't what they were. There were
those that went, you remember, when they dug a trench for
the gas-pipe. Over the fields, and through the wood, and all.
A kind of tunnel it gave them, all the way to Leighton
Buzzard.'

'And what did they find there?' said Pod unkindly. 'A mountain of coke!'

Homily turned away. 'Arrietty,' she said, in the same firm voice, 'supposing one day—we'd pick a special day when there was no one about, and, providing they don't get a cat, which I have my reasons for thinking they won't—supposing, one day, your father took you out borrowing, you'd be a good girl, wouldn't you? You'd do just what he said, quickly and quietly, and no arguing?'

Arrietty turned quite pink; she clasped her hands together. 'Oh—' she began in an ecstatic voice, but Pod cut in quickly: 'Now, Homily, we got to think. You can't just say things like that without thinking it out proper. I been "seen" remember. This is no kind of time for taking a child upstairs.'

'There won't be no cat,' said Homily; 'there wasn't no screeching. It's not like that time with Rosa Pickhatchet.'

'All the same,' said Pod uncertainly, 'the risk's there. I never heard of no *girl* going borrowing before.'

'The way I look at it,' said Homily, 'and it's only now it's come to me: if you had a son, you'd take him borrowing, now, wouldn't you? Well, you haven't got no son—only Arrietty. Suppose anything happened to you or me, where would Arrietty be—if she hadn't learned to borrow?'

Pod stared down at his knees. 'Yes,' he said after a moment, 'I see what you mean.'

'And it'll give her a bit of interest like and stop her hankering.'

'Hankering for what?'

'For blue sky and grass and suchlike.' Arrietty caught her breath and Homily turned on her swiftly: 'It's no good, Arrietty, I'm not going to emigrate—not for you nor anyone else!'

'Ah,' said Pod and began to laugh, 'so that's it!'

'Shush!' said Homily, annoyed, and glanced quickly at the ceiling. 'Not so loud! Now kiss your father, Arrietty,' she went on briskly, 'and pop off back to bed.'

As Arrietty snuggled down under the bedclothes she felt, creeping up from her toes, a glow of happiness like a glow of warmth. She heard their voices rising and falling in the next room: Homily went on and on, measured and confident— there was, Arrietty felt, a kind of conviction behind it; it was the winning voice. Once she heard Pod get up and the scrape of a chair. 'I don't like it!' she heard him say. And she heard Homily whisper 'Hush!' and there were tremulous footfalls on the floor above and the sudden clash of pans.

Arrietty, half dozing, gazed up at her painted ceiling. 'FLOR DE HAVANA' proclaimed the banners proudly. 'Garantizados Superiores... Non Plus Ultra... Esquisitos...' and the lovely gauzy ladies blew their trumpets, silently, triumphantly, on soundless notes of glee.

Chapter Seven

For the next three weeks Arrietty was especially 'good': she helped her mother tidy the store-rooms; she swept and watered the passages and trod them down; she sorted and graded the beads (which they used as buttons) into the screw-tops of aspirin bottles; she cut old kid gloves into squares for Pod's shoemaking; she filed fish-bone needles to a beesting sharpness; she hung up the washing to dry by the grating so that it blew in the soft air; and at last the day came—that dreadful, wonderful, never-to-be-forgotten day—when Homily, scrubbing the kitchen table, straightened her back and called 'Pod!'

He came in from his workroom, last in hand.

'Look at this brush!' cried Homily. It was a fibre brush with a plaited, fibre back.

'Aye,' said Pod, 'worn down.'

'Gets me knuckles now,' said Homily, 'every time I scrub.'

Pod looked worried. Since he had been 'seen', they had stuck to kitchen borrowing, and bare essentials of fuel and food. There was an old mouse-hole under the kitchen stove upstairs which, at night when the fire was out or very low, Pod could use as a chute to save carrying. Since the window-curtain incident they had pushed a match-box chest of drawers below the mouse hole, and had stood a wooden stool on the chest of drawers; and Pod, with much help and shoving from Homily, had learned to squeeze up the chute instead of down. In this way he need not venture into the great hall and passages; he could just nip out, from under the vast black stove in the kitchen for a clove or a carrot or a tasty piece of ham. But it was not a satisfactory arrangement: even when the fire was out, often there were hot ash and cinders under the stove and once, as he emerged, a great brush came at him wielded by Mrs Driver; and he slithered back, on top of Homily, singed, shaken, and coughing dust. Another time, for some reason, the fire had been in full blaze and Pod had arrived suddenly beneath a glowing inferno dropping white hot coals. But usually, at night, the fire was out, and Pod could pick his way through the cinders into the kitchen proper.

'Mrs Driver's out,' Homily went on. 'It's her day off. And She'—they always spoke of Aunt Sophy as 'She'—'is safe enough in bed.'

'It's not them that worries me,' said Pod.

'Why,' exclaimed Homily sharply, 'the boy's not still here?'

'I don't know,' said Pod; 'there's always a risk,' he added.

'And there always will be,' retorted Homily, 'like when you was in the coal-cellar and the coal-cart came.'

'But the other two,' said Pod, 'Mrs Driver and Her, I always know where they are, like.'

'As for that,' exclaimed Homily, 'a boy's even better. You can hear a boy a mile off. Well,' she went on after a moment, 'please yourself. But it's not like you to talk of risks...'

Pod sighed. 'All right,' he said and turned away to fetch his borrowing bag.

'Take the child,' called Homily after him.

Pod turned. 'Now, Homily,' he began in an alarmed voice.

'Why not?' asked Homily sharply. 'It's just the day. You aren't going no farther than the front door. If you're nervous you can leave her by the clock, ready to nip underneath and down the hole. Let her just see at any rate. Arrietty!'

As Arrietty came running in Pod tried again. 'Now listen, Homily—' he protested.

Homily ignored him. 'Arrietty,' she said brightly, 'would you like to go along with your father and borrow me some brush fibre from the door mat in the hall?'

Arrietty gave a little skip. 'Oh,' she cried, 'could I?'

'Well, take your apron off,' said Homily, 'and change your boots. You want light shoes for borrowing—better wear the red kid.' And then as Arrietty spun away Homily turned to Pod: 'She'll be all right,' she said; 'you'll see.'

As she followed her father down the passage Arrietty's heart began to beat faster. Now the moment had come at last she found it almost too much to bear. She felt light and trembly, and hollow with excitement.

They had three borrowing bags between the two of them

('In case,' Pod had explained, 'we pick up something. A bad
Borrower loses many a chance for lack of an extra bag'), and
Pod laid these down to open the first gate, which was latched
by a safety-pin. It was a big pin, too strongly sprung for little
hands to open, and Arrietty watched her father swing his
whole weight on the bar and his feet kick loose off the
ground. Hanging from his hands, he shifted his weight along
the pin towards the curved sheath, and, as he moved, the pin
sprang open and he, in the same instant, jumped free. 'You
couldn't do that,' he remarked, dusting his hands; 'too light.
Nor could your mother. Come along now. Quietly...'

There were other gates; all of which Pod left open ('Never
shut a gate on the way out,' he explained in a whisper, 'you
might need to get back quick') and after a while, Arrietty saw
a faint light at the end of the passage. She pulled her father's
sleeve. 'Is that it?' she whispered.

Pod stood still. 'Quietly, now,' he warned her. 'Yes, that's
it: the hole under the clock!' As he said these words, Arrietty
felt breathless, but outwardly she made no sign. 'There are
three steps up to it,' Pod went on, 'steep like, so mind how
you go. When you're under the clock you just stay there;
don't let your mind wander and keep your eyes on me: if all's
clear, I'll give you the sign.'

The steps were high and a little uneven but Arrietty took
them more lightly than Pod. As she scrambled past the jagged
edges of the hole she had a sudden blinding glimpse of
molten gold: it was spring sunshine on the pale stones of the

hall floor. Standing upright, she could no longer see this; she could only see the cave-like shadows in the great case above her and the dim outline of the hanging weights. The hollow darkness around her vibrated with sound; it was a safe sound—solid and regular; and, far above her head, she saw the movement of the pendulum; it gleamed a little in the half-light, remote and cautious in its rhythmic swing. Arrietty felt warm tears behind her eyelids and a sudden swelling pride: so this, at last, was The Clock! Their clock... after which her family was named! For two hundred years it had stood there, deep-voiced and patient, guarding their threshold, and meas-uring their time.

But Pod, she saw, stood crouched beneath the carved arch-way against the light: 'Keep your eyes on me,' he had said, so Arrietty crouched too. She saw the gleaming golden stone floor of the hall stretching away into distance; she saw the edges of rugs, like richly coloured islands in a molten sea, and she saw, in a glory of sunlight—like a dreamed-of gate-way to fairyland—the open front door. Beyond she saw grass and, against the clear, bright sky, a waving frond of green. Pod's eyes slewed round. 'Wait,' he breathed, 'and watch.' And then in a flash he was gone. Arrietty saw him scurry across the sunlit floor.

Swiftly he ran—as a mouse runs or a blown dry leaf—and suddenly she saw him as 'small'. But she told herself, 'He isn't small. He's half a head taller than mother...' She watched him run round a chestnut-coloured island of doormat into the shadows beside the door. There, it seemed, he became invisible.

Arrietty watched and waited. All was still except for a sudden whirr within the clock. A grinding whirr it was, up high in the hollow darkness above her head, then the sliding grate of slipped metal before the clock sang out its chime. Three notes were struck, deliberate and mellow: 'Take it or leave it,' they seemed to say, 'but that's the time—'

A sudden movement near the shadowed lintel of the front door and there was Pod again, bag in hand, beside the mat; it rose knee deep before him like a field of chestnut corn. Arrietty saw him glance towards the clock and then she saw him raise his hand.

Oh, the warmth of the stone flags as she ran across them... the gladdening sunlight on her face and hands... the awful space above and around her! Pod caught her and held her at last, and patted her shoulder. 'There, there...' he said, 'get your breath—good girl!'

Panting a little, Arrietty gazed about her. She saw great chair legs rearing up into sunlight; she saw the shadowed undersides of their seats spread above her like canopies; she saw the nails and the strapping and odd tags of silk and string; she saw the terraced cliffs of the stairs, mounting up into the distance, up and up... she saw carved table legs and a cavern under the chest. And all the time, in the stillness, the clock spoke—measuring out the seconds, spreading its layers of calm.

And then, turning, Arrietty looked at the garden. She saw a gravelled path, full of coloured stones—the size of walnuts they were, with, here and there, a blade of grass between them, transparent green against the light of the sun. Beyond the path she saw a grassy bank rising steeply to a tangled hedge; and beyond the hedge she saw fruit trees, bright with blossom.

'Here's a bag,' said Pod in a hoarse whisper; 'better get down to work.'

Obediently Arrietty started pulling fibre; stiff it was and full of dust. Pod worked swiftly and methodically, making small bundles, each of which he put immediately in the bag. 'If you have to run suddenly,' he explained, 'you don't want to leave nothing behind.'

'It hurts your hands,' said Arrietty, 'doesn't it?' and suddenly she sneezed.

'Not my hands it doesn't,' said Pod, 'they're hardened like,' and Arrietty sneezed again.

'Dusty, isn't it?' she said.

Pod straightened his back. 'No good pulling where it's knotted right in,' he said, watching her. 'No wonder it hurts your hands. See here,' he exclaimed after a moment, 'you leave it! It's your first time up like. You sit on the step there and take a peek out of doors.'

'Oh, no—' Arrietty began ('If I don't help,' she thought, 'he won't want me again') but Pod insisted.

'I'm better on me own,' he said. 'I can choose me bits, if

you see what I mean, seeing as it's me who's got to make the brush.'

Chapter Eight

The step was warm but very steep. 'If I got down on to the path,' Arrietty thought, 'I might not get up again,' so for some moments she sat quietly. After a while she noticed the shoe-scraper.

'Arrietty,' called Pod softly, 'where have you got to?'

'I just climbed down the shoe-scraper,' she called back.

He came along and looked down at her from the top of the step. 'That's all right,' he said after a moment's stare, 'but never climb down anything that isn't fixed like. Supposing one of them came along and moved the shoe-scraper—where would you be then? How would you get up again?'

'It's heavy to move,' said Arrietty.

'Maybe,' said Pod, 'but it's movable. See what I mean? There's rules, my lass, and you got to learn.'

'This path,' Arrietty said, 'goes round the house. And the bank does too.'

'Well,' said Pod, 'what of it?'

Arrietty rubbed one red kid shoe on a rounded stone. 'It's my grating,' she explained. 'I was thinking that my grating must be just round the corner. My grating looks out on to this bank.'

'Your grating!' exclaimed Pod. 'Since when has it been your grating?'

'I was thinking,' Arrietty went on. 'Suppose I just went round the corner and called through the grating to mother?'

'No,' said Pod, 'we're not going to have none of that. Not going round corners.'

'Then,' went on Arrietty, 'she'd see I was all right.'

'Well,' said Pod, and then he half smiled, 'go quickly then and call. I'll watch for you here. Not loud mind!'

Arrietty ran. The stones in the path were firmly bedded and her light, soft shoes hardly seemed to touch them. How glorious it was to run—you could never run under the floor: you walked, you stooped, you crawled—but you never ran. Arrietty nearly ran past the grating. She saw it just in time after she turned the corner. Yes, there it was quite close to the ground, embedded deeply in the old wall of the house; there was moss below it in a spreading, greenish stain.

Arrietty ran up to it. 'Mother!' she called, her nose against the iron grille. 'Mother!' She waited quietly and, after a moment, she called again.

At the third call Homily came. Her hair was coming down and she carried, as though it were heavy, the screw lid of a pickle jar, filled with soapy water. 'Oh,' she said in an annoyed voice, 'you didn't half give me a turn! What do you think you're up to? Where's your father?'

Arrietty jerked her head sideways. 'Just there—by the front door!' She was so full of happiness that, out of Homily's sight, her toes danced on the green moss. Here she was on the other side of the grating—here she was at last, on the out-side—looking in!

'Yes,' said Homily, 'they open that door like that—the first day of spring. Well,' she went on briskly, 'you run back to your father. And tell him, if the morning-room door happens to be open that I wouldn't say no to a bit of red blotting-paper. Mind out of my way now while I throw the water!'

'That's what grows the moss,' thought Arrietty as she sped back to her father, 'all the water we empty through the grating…'

Pod looked relieved when he saw her but frowned at the message. 'How's she expect me to climb that desk without me pin? Blotting-paper's a curtain-and-chair job and she should know it. Come on now! Up with you!'

'Let me stay down,' pleaded Arrietty, 'just a bit longer. Just till you finish. They're all out. Except Her. Mother said so.'

'She'd say anything,' grumbled Pod, 'when she wants something quick. How does she know. She won't take it into her head to get out of that bed of Hers and come downstairs with a stick? How does she know Mrs Driver ain't stayed at home today—with a headache? How does she know that boy ain't still here?'

'What boy?' asked Arrietty.

Pod looked embarrassed. 'What boy?' he repeated vague-ly and then went on: 'Or maybe Crampfurl—'

'Crampfurl isn't a boy,' said Arrietty.

'No, he isn't,' said Pod, 'not in a manner of speaking. No,' he went on as though thinking this out, 'no, you wouldn't call Crampfurl a boy. Not, as you might say, a boy—exactly. Well,' he said, beginning to move away, 'stay down a bit if you like. But stay close!'

Arrietty watched him move away from the step and then she looked about her. Oh, glory! Oh, joy! Oh, freedom! The sunlight, the grasses, the soft, moving air and half-way up the bank, where it curved round the corner, a flowering cherry-tree! Below it on the path lay a stain of pinkish petals and at the tree's foot, pale as butter, a nest of primroses.

Arrietty threw a cautious glance towards the front door step and then, light and dancey, in her soft red shoes, she ran towards the petals.

They were curved like shells and rocked as she touched them. She gathered several up and laid them one inside the other... up and up... like a card castle. And then she spilled them. Pod came again to the top of the step and looked along the path. 'Don't you go far,' he said after a moment. Seeing his lips move, she smiled back at him: she was too far already to hear the words.

A greenish beetle, shining in the sunlight, came towards her across the stones. She laid her fingers lightly on its shell and it stood still, waiting and watchful, and when she moved her hand the beetle went swiftly on. An ant came hurrying in a busy zig zag. She danced in front of it to tease it and put out

THE BORROWERS

her foot. It stared at her, nonplussed, waving its antennae; then pettishly, as though put out, it swerved away. Two birds came down, quarrelling shrilly, into the grass below the tree. One flew away but Arrietty could see the other among the moving grass stems above her on the slope. Cautiously she moved towards the bank and climbed a little nervously in amongst the green blades. As she parted them gently with her bare hands, drops of water plopped on her skirt and she felt the red shoes become damp. But on she went, pulling herself up now and again by rooty stems into this jungle of moss and wood-violet and creeping leaves of clover. The sharp-seeming grass blades, waist high, were tender to the touch and sprang back lightly behind her as she passed. When at last she reached the foot of the tree, the bird took fright and flew away and she sat down suddenly on a gnarled leaf of primrose. The air was filled with scent. 'But nothing will play with you,' she thought and saw the cracks and furrows of the primrose leaves held crystal beads of dew. If she pressed the leaf these rolled like marbles. The bank was warm, almost too warm here within the shelter of the tall grass, and the sandy earth smelled dry. Standing up, she picked a primrose. The pink stalk felt tender and living in her hands and was covered with silvery hairs, and when she held the flower, like a parasol, between her eyes and the sky, she saw the sun's pale light through the veined petals. On a piece of bark she found a wood-louse and she struck it lightly with her swaying flower. It curled immediately and became a ball, bump-

58

ing softly away downhill in amongst the grass roots. But she knew about wood-lice. There were plenty of them at home under the floor. Homily always scolded her if she played with them because, she said, they smelled of old knives. She lay back among the stalks of the primroses and they made a coolness between her and the sun, and then, sighing, she turned her head and looked sideways up the bank among the grass stems. Startled, she caught her breath. Something had moved above her on the bank. Something had glittered. Arrietty stared.

CHAPTER NINE

It was an eye. Or it looked like an eye. Clear and bright like the colour of the sky. An eye like her own but enormous. A glaring eye. Breathless with fear, she sat up. And the eye blinked. A great fringe of lashes came curving down and flew up again out of sight. Cautiously, Arrietty moved her legs: she would slide noiselessly in among the grass stems and slither away down the bank.

'Don't move!' said a voice, and the voice, like the eye, was enormous but somehow, hushed and hoarse like a surge of wind through the grating on a stormy night in March.

Arrietty froze. 'So this is it,' she thought, 'the worst and most terrible thing of all: I have been "seen"! Whatever happened to Eggletina will now, almost certainly, happen to me!'

There was a pause and Arrietty, her heart pounding in her ears, heard the breath again drawn swiftly into the vast lungs. 'Or' said the voice, whispering still, 'I shall hit you with my ash stick.'

Suddenly Arrietty became calm. 'Why?' she asked. How strange her own voice sounded! Crystal thin and harebell clear, it tinkled on the air.

'In case,' came the surprised whisper at last, 'you ran towards me, quickly, through the grass... in case,' it went on, trembling a little, 'you scrabbled at me with your nasty little hands.'

Arrietty stared at the eye; she held herself quite still. 'Why?' she asked again, and again the word tinkled—icy cold it sounded this time, and needle sharp.

'Things do,' said the voice. 'I've seen them. In India.'

Arrietty thought of her *Gazetteer of the World*.

'You're not in India now,' she pointed out.

'Did you come out of the house?'

'Yes,' said Arrietty.

'From whereabouts in the house?'

Arrietty stared at the eye. 'I'm not going to tell you,' she said at last bravely.

'Then I'll hit you with my ash stick!'

'All right,' said Arrietty, 'hit me!'

'I'll pick you up and break you in half!'

Arrietty stood up. 'All right,' she said and took two paces forward.

There was a sharp grasp and an earthquake in the grass: he spun away from her and sat up, a great mountain in a green jersey. He had fair, straight hair and golden eyelashes. 'Stay where you are!' he cried.

Arrietty stared up at him. So this was 'the boy'! Breathless, she felt, and light with fear. 'I guessed you were about nine,' she gasped after a moment.

He flushed. 'Well, you're wrong, I'm ten.' He looked down at her, breathing deeply. 'How old are you?'

'Fourteen,' said Arrietty. 'Next June,' she added, watching him.

There was silence while Arrietty waited, trembling a little. 'Can you read?' the boy said at last.

'Of course,' said Arrietty. 'Can't you?'

'No,' he stammered. 'I mean—yes. I mean I've just come from India.'

'What's that got to do with it?' asked Arrietty.

'Well, if you're born in India, you're bilingual. And if you're bilingual, you can't read. Not so well.'

Arrietty stared up at him: 'what a monster,' she thought, 'dark against the sky'.

'Do you grow out of it?' she asked.

He moved a little and she felt the cold flick of his shadow.

'Oh yes,' he said, 'it wears off. My sisters were bilingual; now they aren't a bit. They could read any of those books upstairs in the schoolroom.'

'So could I,' said Arrietty quickly, 'if someone could hold them, and turn the pages. I'm not a bit bilingual. I can read anything.'

'Could you read out loud?'

'Of course,' said Arrietty.

'Would you wait here while I run upstairs and get a book now?'

'Well,' said Arrietty; she was longing to show off; then a startled look came into her eyes. 'Oh—' she faltered.

'What's the matter?' The boy was standing up now. He

towered above her.

'How many doors are there to this house?' She squinted up at him against the bright sunlight. He dropped on one knee.

'Doors?' he said. 'Outside doors?'

'Yes.'

'Well, there's the front door, the back door, the gun room door, the kitchen door, the scullery door.... and the french windows in the drawing-room.'

'Well, you see,' said Arrietty 'my father's in the hall, by the front door, working. He... he wouldn't want to be disturbed.'

'Working?' said the boy. 'What at?'

'Getting material,' said Arrietty, 'for a scrubbing-brush.'

'Then I'll go in the side door.' He began to move away but turned suddenly and came back to her. He stood a moment, as though embarrassed, and then he said: 'Can you fly?'

'No,' said Arrietty, surprised; 'can you?'

His face became even redder. 'Of course not,' he said angrily; 'I'm not a fairy!'

'Well, nor am I,' said Arrietty, 'nor is anybody. I don't believe in them.'

He looked at her strangely. 'You don't believe in them?'

'No,' said Arrietty; 'do you?'

'Of course not!'

'Really,' she thought, 'he is a very angry kind of boy'. 'My mother believes in them,' she said, trying to appease him. 'She thinks she saw one once. It was when she was a girl and lived with her parents behind the sand pile in the potting-shed.'

He squatted down on his heels and she felt his breath on her face. 'What was it like?' he asked.

'About the size of a glow-worm with wings like a butterfly. And it had a tiny little face, she said, all alight and moving like sparks and tiny moving hands. Its face was changing all the time, she said, smiling and sort of shimmering. It seemed to be talking, she said, very quickly—but you couldn't hear a word.'

'Oh,' said the boy, interested. After a moment he asked: 'Where did it go?'

'It just went,' said Arrietty. 'When my mother saw it, it seemed to be caught in a cobweb. It was dark at the time. About five o'clock on a winter's evening. After tea.'

'Oh,' he said again and picked up two petals of cherry-blossom which he folded together like a sandwich and ate slowly. 'Supposing,' he said, staring past her at the wall of the house, 'you saw a little man, about as tall as a pencil, with a blue patch on his trousers, half-way up a window curtain, carrying a doll's tea-cup would you say it was a fairy?'

'No,' said Arrietty, 'I'd say it was my father.'

'Oh,' said the boy, thinking this out, 'does your father have a blue patch on his trousers?'

'Not on his best trousers. He does on his borrowing ones.'

'Oh,' said the boy again. He seemed to find it a safe sound, as lawyers do. 'Are there many people like you?'

'No,' said Arrietty. 'None. We're all different.'

'I mean as small as you?'

Arrietty laughed. 'Oh, don't be silly!' she said. 'Surely you don't think there are many people in the world your size?'

'There are more my size than yours,' he retorted.

'Honestly—' began Arrietty helplessly and laughed again. 'Do you really think—I mean, whatever sort of a world would it be? Those great chairs... I've seen them. Fancy if you had to make chairs that size for everyone? And the stuff for their clothes... miles and miles of it... tents of it... and the sewing! And their great houses, reaching up so you can hardly see the ceilings... their great beds... the *food* they eat great, smoking mountains of it, huge bogs of stew and soup and stuff.'

'Don't you eat soup?' asked the boy.

'Of course we do,' laughed Arrietty 'My father had an uncle who had a little boat which he rowed round in the stock-pot picking up flotsam and jetsam. He did bottom-fishing too for bits of marrow until the cook got suspicious through finding bent pins in the soup. Once he was nearly shipwrecked on a chunk of submerged shin-bone. He lost his oars and the boat sprang a leak but he flung a line over the pot handle and pulled himself alongside the rim. But all that stock—fathoms of it! And the size of the stock-pot! I mean, there wouldn't be enough stuff in the world to go round after a bit! That's why my father says it's a good thing they're dying out... just a few, my father says, that's all we need—to keep us. Otherwise he says, the whole thing gets'—Arrietty hesitated, trying to remember the word—'exaggerated, he says—'

'What do you mean,' asked the boy, "to keep us"?'

CHAPTER TEN

So Arrietty told him about borrowing—how difficult it was and how dangerous. She told him about the store-rooms under the floor; about Pod's early exploits, the skill he had shown and the courage; she described those far-off days, before her birth, when Pod and Homily had been rich; she described the musical snuff-box, of gold filigree, and the little bird which flew out of it made of kingfisher feathers, how it flapped its wings and sang its song; she described the doll's wardrobe and the tiny green glasses; the little silver teapot out of the drawing-room case; the satin bedcovers and embroidered sheets... 'those we have still,' she told him, 'they're Her handkerchiefs...' 'She', the boy realized gradually, was his Great Aunt Sophy upstairs; he heard how Pod would borrow from her bedroom, picking his way—in the firelight—among the trinkets on her dressing-table, even climbing her bed-curtains and walking on her quilt. And of how she would watch him and sometimes talk to him because, Arrietty explained, every day at six o'clock they brought her a decanter of Fine Old Pale Madeira, and how before midnight she would drink the lot. Nobody blamed her, not even Homily, because, as Homily would say, 'She' had so few pleasures, poor soul, but, Arrietty explained, after the first three glasses Great Aunt Sophy never believed in anything she saw. 'She thinks my father comes out of the decanter,' said Arrietty, 'and one day when I'm older he's going to take me there and she'll think I come out of the decanter too. It'll please her, my father thinks, as she's used to him now. Once he took my mother, and Aunt Sophy perked up like anything and kept asking why my mother didn't come any more and saying they'd watered the Madeira because once, she says, she saw a little man and a little woman and now she only sees a little man...'

'I wish she thought I came out of the decanter,' said the boy. 'She gives me dictation and teaches me to write. I only see her in the mornings when she's cross. She sends for me and looks behind my ears and asks Mrs D. if I've learned my words.'

'What does Mrs D. look like?' asked Arrietty. (How delicious it was to say 'Mrs D.' like that... how careless and daring!) 'She's fat and has a moustache and gives me my bath and hurts my bruise and my sore elbow and says she'll take a slipper to me one of these days...' The boy pulled up a tuft of grass and stared at it angrily and Arrietty saw his lip tremble. 'My mother's very nice,' he said. 'She lives in India. Why did you lose all your worldly riches?'

'Well,' said Arrietty, 'the kitchen boiler burst and hot water came pouring through the floor into our house and everything was washed away and piled up in front of the grating. My father worked night and day. First hot, then cold.

Trying to salvage things. And there's a dreadful draught in March through that grating. He got ill, you see, and couldn't go borrowing. So my Uncle Hendreary had to do it and one or two others and my mother gave them things bit by bit, for all their trouble. But the kingfisher bird was spoilt by the water; all its feathers fell off and a great twirly spring came jumping out of its side. My father used the spring to keep the door shut against draughts from the grating and my mother put the feathers in a little moleskin hat. After a while I got born and my father went borrowing again. But he gets tired now and doesn't like curtains, not when any of the bobbles are off...'

'I helped him a bit,' said the boy, 'with the tea-cup. He was shivering all over. I suppose he was frightened.'

'My father frightened!' exclaimed Arrietty angrily. 'Frightened of you!' she added.

'Perhaps he doesn't like heights,' said the boy.

'He loves heights,' said Arrietty. 'The thing he doesn't like is curtains. I've told you. Curtains make him tired.'

The boy sat thoughtfully on his haunches, chewing a blade of grass. 'Borrowing,' he said after a while. 'Is that what you call it?'

'What else could you call it?' asked Arrietty.

'I'd call it stealing.'

Arrietty laughed. She really laughed. 'But we are Borrowers,' she explained, 'like you're a—a Human Bean or whatever it's called. We're part of the house. You might as well say that the fire-grate steals the coal from the coal-scuttle.'

'Then what is stealing?'

Arrietty looked grave. 'Supposing my Uncle Hendreary borrowed an emerald watch from Her dressing-table and my father took it and hung it up on our wall. That's stealing.'

'An emerald watch!' exclaimed the boy.

'Well, I just said that because we have one on the wall at home, but my father borrowed it himself. It needn't be a watch. It could be anything. A lump of sugar, even. But Borrowers don't steal.'

'Except from human beans,' said the boy.

Arrietty burst out laughing; she laughed so much that she had to hide her face in the primrose. 'Oh dear,' she gasped with tears in her eyes, 'you are funny!' She stared upwards at his puzzled face. 'Human beans are *for* Borrowers—like bread's for butter!'

The boy was silent a while. A sigh of wind rustled the cherry-tree and shivered among the blossom.

'Well, I don't believe it,' he said at last, watching the falling petals. 'I don't believe that's what we're for at all and I don't believe we're dying out!'

'Oh, goodness!' exclaimed Arrietty impatiently, staring up at his chin. 'Just use your common sense: you're the only real human bean I ever saw (although I do just know of three more—Crampfurl, Her, and Mrs Driver). But I know lots and lots of Borrowers: the Overmantels and the Harpsichords and the Rain-Barrels and the Linen-Presses and the Boot-Racks and the Hon. John Studdingtons and—'

He looked down. 'John Studdington? But he was our grand uncle—'

'Well, this family lived behind a picture,' went on Arrietty, hardly listening, 'and there were the Stove-Pipes and the Bell-Pulls and the—'

'Yes,' he interrupted, 'but did you see them?'

'I saw the Harpsichords. And my mother was a Bell-Pull. The others were before I was born...' He leaned closer 'Then where are they now? Tell me that.'

'My Uncle Hendreary has a house in the country' said Arrietty coldly, edging away from his great lowering face; it was misted over, she noticed, with hairs of palest gold. 'And five children, Harpsichords and Clocks.'

'But where are the others?'

'Oh,' said Arrietty, 'they're somewhere.' But where? she wondered. And she shivered slightly in the boy's cold shadow, which lay about her, slant-wise, on the grass.

He drew back again, his fair head blocking out a great piece of sky. 'Well,' he said deliberately after a moment, and his eyes were cold, 'I've only seen two Borrowers but I've seen hundreds and hundreds and hundreds and hundreds and hundreds—'

'Oh no—' whispered Arrietty.

'Of human beans.' And he sat back.

Arrietty stood very still. She did not look at him. After a

71

while she said: 'I don't believe you.'

'All right,' he said, 'then I'll tell you—'

'I still won't believe you,' murmured Arrietty.

'Listen!' he said. And he told her about railway stations and football matches and racecourses and royal processions and Albert Hall concerts. He told her about India and China and North America and the British Commonwealth. He told her about the July sales. 'Not hundreds,' he said, 'but thousands and millions and billions and trillions of great, big, enormous people. Now do you believe me?'

Arrietty stared up at him with frightened eyes: it gave her a crick in the neck. 'I don't know,' she whispered.

'As for you,' he went on, leaning closer again, 'I don't believe that there are any more Borrowers anywhere in the world. I believe you're the last three,' he said.

Arrietty dropped her face into the primrose. 'We're not. There's Aunt Lupy and Uncle Hendreary and all the cousins.'

'I bet they're dead,' said the boy. 'And what's more,' he went on, 'no one will ever believe I've seen you. And you'll be the very last because you're the youngest. One day,' he told her, smiling triumphantly, 'you'll be the only Borrower left in the world!'

He sat still, waiting, but she did not look up. 'Now you're crying,' he remarked after a moment.

'They're not dead,' said Arrietty in a muffled voice: she was feeling in her little pocket for a handkerchief. 'They live in a badger's set two fields away, beyond the spinney. We don't see them because it's too far. There are weasels and things and cows and foxes... and crows...'

'Which spinney?' he asked.

'I don't KNOW!' Arrietty almost shouted. 'It's along by the gas-pipe—a field called Parkin's Beck.' She blew her nose. 'I'm going home,' she said.

'Don't go,' he said, 'not yet.'

'Yes, I'm going,' said Arrietty.

His face turned pink. 'Let me just get the book,' he pleaded.

'I'm not going to read to you now,' said Arrietty.

'Why not?'

She looked at him with angry eyes. 'Because—'

'Listen,' he said, 'I'll go to that field. I'll go and find Uncle Hendreary. And the cousins. And Aunt What-ever-she-is. And, if they're alive, I'll tell you. What about that? You could write them a letter and I'd put it down the hole—'

Arrietty gazed up at him: 'Would you?' she breathed.

'Yes, I would. Really I would. Now can I go and get the book? I'll go in by the side door.'

'All right,' said Arrietty absently. Her eyes were shining. 'When can I give you the letter?'

'Any time,' he said, standing above her. 'Where in the house do you live?'

'Well—' began Arrietty and stopped. Why once again did she feel this chill? Could it only be his shadow... towering above her, blotting out the sun? 'I'll put it somewhere,' she said hurriedly, 'I'll put it under the hall mat.'

'Which one? The one by the front door?'

'Yes, that one.'

He was gone. And she stood there alone in the sunshine, shoulder deep in grass. What had happened seemed too big for thought; she felt unable to believe it really had happened: not only had she been 'seen' but she had been talked to; not only had she been talked to but she had— 'Arrietty!' said a voice.

She stood up, startled, and spun round: there was Pod, moon-faced, on the path looking up at her. 'Come on down!' he whispered.

She stared at him for a moment as though she did not recognize him; how round his face was, how kind, how familiar!

'Come on!' he said again, more urgently; and obediently, because he sounded worried, she slithered quickly towards him off the bank, balancing her primrose. 'Put that thing down,' he said sharply, when she stood at last beside him on the path. 'You can't lug great flowers about—you got to carry a bag. What you want to go up there for?' he grumbled as they moved off across the stones. 'I might never have seen you. Hurry up now. Your mother'll have tea waiting!'

CHAPTER ELEVEN

Homily was there, at the last gate, to meet them. She had tidied her hair and smelled of coal-tar soap. She looked younger and somehow excited. 'Well—!' she kept saying. 'Well!' taking the bag from Arrietty and helping Pod to fasten the gate. 'Well, was it nice? Were you a good girl? Was the cherry-tree out? Did the clock strike?' She seemed, in the dim light, to be trying to read the expression on Arrietty's face. 'Come along now. Tea's all ready. Give me your hand...'

Tea was indeed ready, laid on the round table in the sitting-room with a bright fire burning in the cog-wheel. How familiar the room seemed, and homely, but, suddenly, somehow strange; the firelight flickering on the wall-paper—the line which read: '... it would be so charming if—'. If what? Arrietty always wondered. If our house were less dark, she thought, that would be charming. She looked at the home-made dips set in upturned drawing-pins which Homily had placed as candleholders among the tea things; the old teapot, a hollow oak-apple, with its quill spout and wired-on handle—burnished it was now and hard with age; there were two roast sliced chestnuts which they would eat like toast with butter and a cold boiled chestnut which Pod would cut like bread; there was a plate of hot dried currants, well plumped before the fire; there were cinnamon breadcrumbs, crispy golden, and lightly dredged with sugar, and in front of each place, oh, delight of delights, a single potted shrimp. Homily had put out the silver plates—the florin ones for herself and Arrietty and the half-crown one for Pod.

'Come along, Arrietty, if you've washed your hands,' exclaimed Homily, taking up the teapot, 'don't dream!'

Arrietty drew up a cotton-reel and sat down slowly. She watched her mother pulling on the spout of the teapot; this was always an interesting moment. The thicker end of the quill being inside the teapot, a slight pull just before pouring would draw it tightly into the hole and thus prevent a leak. If, as sometimes happened, a trace of dampness appeared about the join, it only meant a rather harder pull and a sudden gentle twist.

'Well?' said Homily, gingerly pouring. 'Tell us what you saw!'

'She didn't see so much,' said Pod, cutting himself a slice of boiled chestnut to eat with his shrimp.

'Didn't she see the overmantel?'

'No,' said Pod, 'we never went in the morning-room.'

'What about my blotting-paper?'

'I never got it,' said Pod.

'Now that's a nice thing—' began Homily.

'Maybe,' said Pod, munching steadily, 'but I had me feeling. I had it bad.'

'What's that?' asked Arrietty. 'His feeling?'

'Up the back of his head and in his fingers,' said Homily. 'It's a feeling your father gets when'—she dropped her voice—'there's someone about.'

'Oh,' said Arrietty and seemed to shrink.

'That's why I brought her along home,' said Pod.

'And was there anyone?' asked Homily anxiously.

Pod took a mouthful of shrimp. 'Must have been,' he said, 'but I didn't see nothing.'

Homily leaned across the table. 'Did you have any feeling, Arrietty?'

Arrietty started. 'Oh,' she said, 'do we all have it?'

'Well, not in the same place,' said Homily 'Mine starts at the back of me ankles and then me knees go. My mother—hers used to start just under her chin and run right round her neck—'

'And tied in a bow at the back,' said Pod, munching.

'No, Pod,' protested Homily, 'it's a fact. No need to be sarcastic. All the Bell-pulls were like that. Like a collar, she said it was—'

'Pity it didn't choke her,' said Pod.

'Now, Pod, be fair; she had her points.'

'Points!' said Pod. 'She was all points!'

Arrietty moistened her lips; she glanced nervously from Pod to Homily. 'I didn't feel anything,' she said.

'Well,' said Homily, 'perhaps it was a false alarm.'

'Oh no,' began Arrietty, 'it wasn't—' and, as Homily

glanced at her sharply, she faltered: 'I mean if papa felt something—I mean—Perhaps,' she went on, 'I don't have it.'

'Well,' said Homily, 'you're young. It'll come, all in good time. You go and stand in our kitchen, just under the chute, when Mrs Driver's raking out the stove upstairs. Stand right up on a stool or something—so's you're fairly near the ceiling. It'll come—with practice.'

After tea, when Pod had gone to his last and Homily was washing up, Arrietty rushed to her diary: 'I'll just open it,' she thought, trembling with haste, 'anywhere.' It fell open at 9 and 10 July: 'Talk of Camps but Stay at Home. Old Cameronian Colours in Glasgow Cathedral, 1885'— that's what it said for the 9th. And on the 10th the page was headed: 'Make Hay while the Sun Shines. Snowdon Peak sold for £5,750, 1889.' Arrietty tore out this last page. Turning it over she read on the reverse side: '11 July: Make Not a Toil of your Pleasure. Niagara passed by C. D. Graham in a cask, 1886.' No, she thought I'll choose the 10th, 'Make Hay while the Sun Shines' and crossing out her last entry ('Mother out of sorts'), she wrote below it:

Dear Uncle Hendreary,

I hope you are quite well and the cousins are well and Aunt Lupy. We are very well and I am learning to borrow.

Your loving niece,

Arrietty Clock.

Write a letter on the back, please.

xxoxoxx

'What are you doing, Arrietty?' called Homily from the kitchen.

'Writing in my diary'

'Oh,' said Homily shortly.

'Anything you want?' asked Arrietty.

'It'll do later,' said Homily.

Arrietty folded the letter and placed it carefully between the pages of Bryce's *Tom Thumb Gazetteer of the World* and, in the diary, she wrote: 'Went borrowing. Wrote to H. Talked to B.' After that Arrietty sat for a long time staring into the fire, and thinking and thinking and thinking...

CHAPTER TWELVE

But it was one thing to write a letter and quite another to find some means of getting it under the mat. Pod, for several days, could not be persuaded to go borrowing: he was well away on his yearly turn-out of the store-rooms, mending partitions, and putting up new shelves. Arrietty usually enjoyed this spring sorting, when half-forgotten treasures came to light and new uses were discovered for old borrowings. She used to love turning over the scraps of silk or lace; the odd kid gloves; the pencil stubs; the rusty razor blades; the hairpins and the needles; the dried figs, the hazel-nuts, the powdery bits of chocolate, and the scarlet stubs of sealing-wax. Pod, one year, had made her a hairbrush from a toothbrush, and Homily had made her a small pair of Turkish bloomers from two glove fingers for 'knocking about in the mornings'. There were reels and reels of coloured silks and cottons and small variegated balls of odd wool, pen-nibs which Homily used as flour-scoops, and bottle-tops galore.

But this year Arrietty banged about impatiently and stole away whenever she dared, to stare through the grating, hoping to see the boy. She now kept the letter always with her, stuffed inside her jersey, and the edges became rubbed. Once he did run past the grating and she saw his woollen stockings;

he was making a chugging noise in his throat like some kind of engine, and as he turned the corner he let out a piercing 'Ooooo—oo' (it was a train whistle, he told her afterwards) so he did not hear her call. One evening, after dark, she crept away and tried to open the first gate, but swing and tug as she might she could not budge the pin.

Homily, every time she swept the sitting-room, would grumble about the carpet. 'It may be a curtain-and-chair job,' she would say to Pod, 'but it wouldn't take you not a quarter of an hour, with your pin and name-tape, to fetch me a bit of blotting-paper from the desk in the morning-room... anyone would think, looking at this floor, that we lived in a toad-hole. No one could call me house-proud,' said Homily. 'You couldn't be, not with my kind of family, but I do like,' she said, 'to keep "nice things nice".' And at last, on the fourth day, Pod gave in. He laid down his hammer (a small electric bell clapper) and said to Arrietty: 'Come along...'

Arrietty was glad to see the morning-room; the door luckily had been left ajar and it was fascinating to stand at last in the thick pile of the carpet gazing upwards at the shelves and pillars and towering gables of the famous overmantel. So that's where they had lived, she thought, those pleasure loving creatures, remote and gay and self-sufficient. She imagined the Overmantel women—a little 'tweedy', Homily had described them, with wasp waists and piled Edwardian hair—swinging carelessly outwards on the pilasters, lissom and laughing; gazing at themselves in the inset looking-glass which reflected back the tobacco jars, the cut-glass decanters, the bookshelves, and the plush-covered table. She imagined the Overmantel men—fair, they were said to be, with long moustaches and nervous, slender hands— smoking and drinking and telling their witty tales. So they had never asked Homily up there! Poor Homily with her bony nose and never tidy hair... They would have looked at her strangely, Arrietty thought, with their long, half-laughing eyes, and smiled a little and, humming, turned away. And they had lived only on breakfast food—on toast and egg and tiny snips of mushroom; sausage they'd have had and crispy bacon and little sips of tea and coffee. Where were they now? Arrietty wondered. Where could such creatures go?

Pod had flung his pin so it stuck into the seat of the chair and was up the leg in a trice, leaning outwards on his tape; then, pulling out the pin, he flung it like a javelin, above his head, into a fold of curtain. This is the moment, Arrietty thought, and felt for her precious letter. She slipped into the hall. It was darker, this time, with the front door closed, and she ran across it with a beating heart. The mat was heavy, but she lifted up the corner and slid the letter under by pushing with her foot. 'There!' she said, and looked about her... shadows, shadows, and the ticking clock. She looked across the great plain of floor to where, in the distance, the stairs mounted. 'Another world above,' she thought, 'world on world...' and shivered slightly.

'Arrietty,' called Pod softly from the morning-room, and she ran back in time to see him swing clear of the chair seat and pull himself upwards on the name-tape, level with the desk. Lightly he came down feet apart and she saw him, for safety's sake, twist the name-tape lightly round his wrist. 'I wanted you to see that,' he said, a little breathless. The blotting-paper, when he pushed it, floated down quite softly, riding lightly on the air, and lay at last some feet beyond the desk, pink and fresh, on the carpet's dingy pile.

'You start rolling,' whispered Pod. 'I'll be down,' and Arrietty went on her knees and began to roll the blotting-paper until it grew too stiff for her to hold. Pod soon finished it off and lashed it with his name-tape, through which he ran his hat-pin, and together they carried the long cylinder, as two house-painters would carry a ladder, under the clock and down the hole.

Homily hardly thanked them when, panting a little, they dropped the bundle in the passage outside the sitting-room door. She looked alarmed. 'Oh, there you are,' she said. 'Thank goodness! That boy's about again. I've just heard Mrs Driver talking to Crampfurl.'

'Oh!' cried Arrietty. 'What did she say?' and Homily glanced sharply at her and saw that she looked pale. Arrietty realized she should have said: 'What boy?' It was too late now.

'Nothing real bad,' Homily went on, as though to reassure her. 'It's just a boy they have upstairs. It's nothing at all, but

I heard Mrs Driver say that she'd take a slipper to him, see if she wouldn't, if he had the mats up once again in the hall.'

'The mats up in the hall!' echoed Arrietty.

'Yes. Three days running, she said to Crampfurl, he'd had the mats up in the hall. She could tell, she said, by the dust and the way he'd put them back. It was the hall part that worried me, seeing as you and your father—What's the matter, Arrietty? There's no call for that sort of face! Come on now, help me move the furniture and we'll get down the carpet.'

'Oh dear, oh dear,' thought Arrietty miserably, as she helped her mother empty the match-box chest of drawers. 'Three days running he's looked and nothing there. He'll give up hope now... he'll never look again.'

That evening she stood for hours on a stool under the chute in their kitchen, pretending she was practising to get 'a feeling' when really she was listening to Mrs Driver's conversations with Crampfurl. All she learned was that Mrs Driver's feet were killing her, and that it was a pity that she hadn't given in her notice last May, and would Crampfurl have another drop, considering there was more in the cellar than anyone would drink in Her lifetime, and if they thought she was going to clean the first-floor windows single-handed they had better think again. But on the third night, just as Arrietty had climbed down off the stool before she overbalanced with weariness, she heard Crampfurl say: 'If you ask me, I'd say he had a ferret.' And quickly Arrietty climbed back again, holding her breath.

'A ferret!' she heard Mrs Driver exclaim shrilly. 'Whatever next? Where would he keep it?'

'That I wouldn't like to say,' said Crampfurl in his rumbling earthy voice; 'all I know is he was up beyond Parkin's Beck, going round all the banks and calling like down all the rabbit-holes.'

'Well, I never,' said Mrs Driver. 'Where's your glass?'

'Just a drop,' said Crampfurl. 'That's enough. Goes to your liver, this sweet stuff—not like beer, it isn't. Yes,' he went on, 'when he saw me coming with a gun he pretended to be cutting a stick like from the hedge. But I'd see'd him all right and heard him. Calling away, his nose down a rabbit-hole. It's my belief he's got a ferret.' There was a gulp, as through Crampfurl was drinking. 'Yes,' he said at last, and Arrietty heard him set down the glass, 'a ferret called Uncle something.'

Arrietty made a sharp movement, balanced for one moment with arms waving, and fell off the stool. There was a clatter as the stool slid sideways, banged against a chest of drawers and rolled over.

'What was that?' asked Crampfurl.

There was silence upstairs and Arrietty held her breath.

'I didn't hear nothing,' said Mrs Driver.

'Yes,' said Crampfurl, 'it was under the floor like, there by the stove.'

'That's nothing,' said Mrs Driver. 'It's the coals falling. Often sounds like that. Scares you sometimes when you're sitting here alone… Here, pass your glass, there's only a drop left might as well finish the bottle…'

They're drinking Fine Old Madeira, thought Arrietty, and very carefully she set the stool upright and stood quietly beside it, looking up. She could see light through the crack, occasionally flicked with shadow as one person or another moved a hand or arm.

'Yes,' went on Crampfurl, returning to his story, 'and when I come up with m'gun he says, all innocent like—to put me off, I shouldn't wonder: "Any old badgers' sets round here?"'

'Artful,' said Mrs Driver; 'the things they think of… badgers' sets…' and she gave her creaking laugh.

'As a matter of fact,' said Crampfurl, 'there did used to be one, but when I showed him where it was like he didn't take no notice of it. Just stood there, waiting for me to go.' Crampfurl laughed. 'Two can play at that game, I thought, so I just sits m'self down. And there we were the two of us.'

'And what happened?'

'Well, he had to go off in the end. Leaving his ferret. I waited a bit, but it never came out. I poked around a bit and whistled. Pity I never heard properly what he called it. Uncle something it sounded like—' Arrietty heard the sudden scrape of a chair. 'Well,' said Crampfurl, 'I'd better get on now and shut up the chickens—'

The scullery door banged and there was a sudden clatter overhead as Mrs Driver began to rake the stove. Arrietty replaced the stool and stole softly into the sitting-room, where she found her mother alone.

Chapter Thirteen

Homily was ironing, bending and banging and pushing the hair back out of her eyes. All round the room underclothes hung airing on safety-pins, which Homily used like coat-hangers.

'What happened?' asked Homily. 'Did you fall over?'

'Yes,' said Arrietty, moving quietly into her place beside the fire.

'How's the feeling coming?'

'Oh, I don't know,' said Arrietty. She clasped her knees and laid her chin on them.

'Where's your knitting?' asked Homily. 'I don't know what's come over you lately. Always idle. You don't feel seedy, do you?'

'Oh,' exclaimed Arrietty, 'let me be!' And Homily for once was silent. 'It's the spring,' she told herself. 'Used to take me like that sometimes at her age.'

'I must see that boy,' Arrietty was thinking staring blindly into the fire. 'I must hear what happened. I must hear if they're all right. I don't want us to die out. I don't want to be the last Borrower. I don't want'—and here Arrietty dropped her face on to her knees—'to live for ever and ever like this... in the dark... under the floor...'

'No good getting supper,' said Homily, breaking the silence; 'your father's gone borrowing. To Her room. And you know what that means!'

Arrietty raised her head. 'No,' she said, hardly listening; 'what does it mean?'

'That he won't be back,' said Homily sharply, 'for a good hour and a half. He likes it up there, gossiping with Her and poking about on the dressing-table. And it's safe enough once that boy's in bed. Not that there's anything we want special,' she went on. 'It's just these new shelves he's made. They look kind of bare, he says, and he might, he says, just pick up a little something...' Arrietty suddenly was sitting bolt upright: a thought had struck her, leaving her breathless and a little shaky at the knees. 'A good hour and a half,' her mother had said and the gates would be open!

'Where are you going?' asked Homily as Arrietty moved towards the door.

'Just along to the store-rooms,' said Arrietty, shading with one hand her candle-tip from the draught. 'I won't be long.'

'Now don't you untidy anything!' Homily called out after her. 'And be careful of that light!'

As Arrietty went down the passage she thought: 'It is true. I am going to the store-rooms—to find another hat-pin. And if I do find a hat-pin (and a piece of string—there won't be any name-tape) I still "won't be long" because I'll have to get back before papa. And I'm doing it for their sakes,' she told herself doggedly, 'and one day they'll thank me.' All the same she felt a little guilty. 'Artful'—that's what Mrs Driver would say she was.

There was a hat-pin—one with a bar for a top—and she tied on a piece of string, very firmly, twisting it back and forth like a figure of eight and, as a crowning inspiration, she sealed it with sealing-wax.

The gates were open and she left the candle in the middle of the passage where it could come to no harm, just below the hole by the clock.

The great hall when she had climbed out into it was dim with shadows. A single gas jet, turned low, made a pool of light beside the locked front door and another faintly flickered on the landing half-way up the stairs. The ceiling sprang away into height and darkness and all around was space. The night-nursery, she knew, was at the end of the upstairs passage and the boy would be in bed—her mother had just said so.

Arrietty had watched her father use his pin on the chair and single stairs, in comparison, were easier. There was a kind of rhythm to it after a while: a throw, a pull, a scramble, and an upward swing. The stair rods glinted coldly, but the pile of the carpet seemed soft and warm and delicious to fall back on. On the half landing she paused to get her breath. She did not mind the semi-darkness; she lived in darkness; she was at home in it and, at a time like this, it made her feel safe.

On the upper landing she saw an open door and a great

square of golden light which like a barrier lay across the passage. 'I've got to pass through that,' Arrietty told herself, trying to be brave. Inside the lighted room a voice was talking, droning on. '... And this mare,' the voice said, 'was a five-year-old which really belonged to my brother in Ireland, not my elder brother but my younger brother, the one who owned Stale Mate and Oh My Darling. He had entered her for several point-to-points... but when I say "several" I mean three or at least two... Have you ever seen an Irish point-to-point?'

'No,' said another voice, rather absentmindedly. 'That's my father,' Arrietty realized with a start, 'my father talking to Great Aunt Sophy or rather Great Aunt Sophy talking to my father.' She gripped her pin with its loops of string, and ran into the light and through it to the passage beyond. As she passed the open door she had a glimpse of firelight and lamp-light and gleaming furniture and dark-red silk brocade.

Beyond the square of light the passage was dark again and she could see, at the far end, a half-open door. 'That's the day-nursery,' she thought, 'and beyond that is the night-nursery.'

'There are certain differences,' Aunt Sophy's voice went on, 'which would strike you at once. For instance...' Arrietty liked the voice. It was comforting and steady, like the sound of the clock in the hall, and as she moved off the carpet on to the strip of polished floor beside the skirting board, she was interested to hear there were walls in Ireland instead of hedges. Here by the skirting she could run and she loved running. Carpets were heavy going—thick and clinging, they held you up. The boards were smooth and smelled of beeswax.

She liked the smell.

The schoolroom, when she reached it, was shrouded in dust sheets and full of junk. Here, too, a gas jet burned, turned low to a bluish flame. The floor was oil-cloth, rather worn, and the rugs were shabby. Under the table was a great cavern of darkness. She moved into it, feeling about, and bumped into a dusty hassock higher than her head. Coming out again, into the half-light, she looked up and saw the corner cupboard with the doll's tea-service, the painting above the fire-place, and the plush curtain where her father had been 'seen'. Chair legs were everywhere and chair seats obscured her view. She found her way among them to the door of the night-nursery, and there she saw, suddenly, on a shadowed plateau in the far corner, the boy in bed. She saw his great face, turned towards her on the edge of the pillow; she saw the gaslight reflected in his open eyes; she saw his hand gripping the bed-clothes, holding them tightly pressed against his mouth.

She stopped moving and stood still. After a while, when she saw his fingers relax, she said softly: 'Don't be frightened... It's me, Arrietty.' He let the bed clothes slide away from his mouth and said: 'Arri-*what*-y?' He seemed annoyed.

'Etty,' she repeated gently. 'Did you take the letter?'

He stared at her for a moment without speaking, then he

said, 'Why did you come creeping, creeping, into my room?'

'I didn't come creeping, creeping,' said Arrietty. 'I even ran. Didn't you see?'

He was silent, staring at her with his great, wide-open eyes.

'When I brought the book,' he said at last, 'you'd gone.'

'I had to go. Tea was ready. My father fetched me.'

He understood this. 'Oh,' he said matter of factly, and did not reproach her.

'Did you take the letter?' she asked again.

'Yes,' he said, 'I had to go back twice. I shoved it down the badger's hole...' Suddenly he threw back the bed-clothes and stood up in bed, enormous in his pale flannel night-shirt. It was Arrietty's turn to be afraid. She half turned, her eyes on his face, and began backing slowly towards the door. But he did not look at her; he was feeling behind a picture on the wall. 'Here it is,' he said, sitting down again, and the bed creaked loudly.

'But I don't want it back!' exclaimed Arrietty, coming forward again. 'You should have left it there! Why did you bring it back?'

He turned it over in his fingers. 'He's written on it,' he said.

'Oh, please,' cried Arrietty excitedly, 'show me!' She ran right up to the bed and tugged at the trailing sheet. 'Then they are alive! Did you see him?'

'No,' he said, 'the letter was there, just down the hole

where I'd put it.' He leaned towards her. 'But he's written on it. Look!'

She made a quick dart and almost snatched the letter out of his great fingers, but was careful to keep out of range of his grasp. She ran with it to the door of the schoolroom where the light, though dim, was a little brighter. 'It's very faint,' she said, holding it close to her eyes. 'What's he written it with? I wonder. It's all in capitals—' She turned suddenly. 'Are you sure you didn't write it?' she asked.

'Of course not,' he began. 'I write small—' But she had seen by his face that he spoke the truth and began to spell out the letters. 'T—e—double l,' she said. 'Tell y—o—r—e.' She looked up. 'Yore?' she said.

'Yes,' said the boy, 'your.'

'Tell your a—n—t, ant?' said Arrietty. 'Ant? My ant?' The boy was silent, waiting. 'Ant L—u— Oh, Aunt Lupy!' she exclaimed. 'He says listen, this is what he says: "Tell your Aunt Lupy to come home"!'

There was silence. 'Then tell her,' said the boy after a moment.

'But she isn't here!' exclaimed Arrietty. 'She's never been here! I don't even remember what she looked like!'

'Look,' said the boy, staring through the door, 'someone's coming!'

Arrietty whipped round. There was no time to hide: it was Pod, borrowing-bag in one hand and pin in the other. He stood in the doorway of the schoolroom. Quite still he stood, outlined against the light in the passage, his little shadow falling dimly in front of him. He had seen her.

'I heard your voice,' he said, and there was a dreadful quietness about the way he spoke, 'just as I was coming out of Her room.' Arrietty stared back at him, stuffing the letter up her jersey. Could he see beyond her into the shadowed room? Could he see the tousled shape in bed? 'Come on home,' said Pod, and turned away.

CHAPTER FOURTEEN

Pod did not speak until they reached the sitting-room. Nor did he look at her. She had had to scramble after him as best she might. He had ignored her efforts to help him shut the gates, but once, when she tripped, he had waited until she had got up again, watching her, it seemed, almost without interest while she brushed the dust off her knees.

Supper was laid and the ironing put away and Homily came running in from the kitchen, surprised to see them together.

Pod threw down his borrowing bag. He stared at his wife.

'What's the matter?' faltered Homily, looking from one to the other.

'She was in the night-nursery,' said Pod quietly, 'talking to that boy!'

Homily moved forward, her hands clasped tremblingly against her apron, her startled eyes flicking swiftly to and fro. 'Oh, no—' she breathed.

Pod sat down. He ran a tired hand over his eyes and forehead; his face looked heavy like a piece of dough. 'Now what?' he said.

Homily stood quite still; bowed she stood over her clasped hands and stared at Arrietty. 'Oh, you never—' she whispered.

'They are frightened,' Arrietty realized; 'they are not angry at all—they are very, very frightened.' She moved forward. 'It's all right—' she began.

Homily sat down suddenly on the cotton-reel; she had begun to tremble. 'Oh,' she said, 'whatever shall we do?' She began to rock herself, very slightly, to and fro.

'Oh, Mother, don't!' pleaded Arrietty. 'It isn't so bad as that. It really isn't.' She felt up the front of her jersey; at first she could not find the letter—it had slid round her side to the back but at last she drew it out, very crumpled. 'Look,' she said, 'here's a letter from Uncle Hendreary. I wrote to him and the boy took the letter—'

'You wrote to him!' cried Homily on a kind of suppressed shriek. 'Oh,' she moaned, and closed her eyes, 'whatever next! Whatever shall we do?' and she fanned herself limply with her bony hand.

'Get your mother a drink of water, Arrietty,' said Pod sharply. Arrietty brought it in a sawn-off hazel shell—it had been sawn off at the pointed end and was shaped like a brandy glass.

'But whatever made you do such a thing, Arrietty?' said Homily more calmly, setting the empty cup down on the table. 'Whatever came over you?'

So Arrietty told them about being 'seen' that morning under the cherry-tree. And how she had kept it from them not to worry them. And what the boy said about 'dying out'. And how—more than important—how imperative it had seemed to make sure the Hendrearys were alive. 'Do understand,' pleaded Arrietty 'please understand! I'm trying to save the race!'

'The expressions she uses!' said Homily to Pod under her breath, not without pride.

But Pod was not listening. 'Save the race!' he repeated grimly: 'It's people like you, my girl, who do things sudden like with no respect for tradition, who'll finish us Borrowers once for all. Don't you see what you've done?'

Arrietty met his accusing eyes. 'Yes,' she said falteringly, 'I've—I've got in touch with the only other ones still alive. So that,' she went on bravely, 'from now on we can all stick together...'

'All stick together!' Pod repeated angrily. 'Do you think Hendreary's lot would ever come to live back here? Can you see your mother emigrating to a badger's set, two fields away, out in the open and no hot water laid on?'

'Never!' cried Homily in a full, rich voice which made them both turn and look at her.

'Or do you see your mother walking across two fields and a garden,' went on Pod, 'two fields full of crows and cows and horses and what not, to take a cup of tea with your Aunt Lupy, whom she never liked much anyway? But wait,' he said as Arrietty tried to speak, 'that's not the point—as far as all that goes we're just where we was—the point,' he went on, leaning forward and speaking with great solemnity, 'is this: that boy knows now where we live!'

'Oh no,' said Arrietty 'I never told him that. I—'

'You told him,' interrupted Pod, 'about the kitchen pipe bursting; you told him how all our stuff got washed away to the grating.' He sat back again glaring at her. 'He's only got to think,' he pointed out. Arrietty was silent and Pod went on: 'That's a thing that has never happened before, never, in the whole long history of the Borrowers. Borrowers have been "seen"—yes; Borrowers have been caught—maybe: but no human bean has ever known where any Borrower lived. We're in very grave danger, Arrietty, and you've put us there. And that's a fact.'

'Oh, Pod,' whimpered Homily, 'don't frighten the child.'

'Nay, Homily,' said Pod more gently, 'my poor old girl! I don't want to frighten no one, but this is serious. Suppose I said to you pack up tonight, all our bits and pieces, where would you go?'

'Not to Hendreary's,' cried Homily, 'not there, Pod! I couldn't never share a kitchen with Lupy—'

'No,' agreed Pod, 'not to Hendreary's. And don't you see for why? The boy knows about that too!'

'Oh!' cried Homily in real dismay.

'Yes,' said Pod, 'a couple of smart terriers or a well-trained ferret, and that'd be the end of that lot.'

'Oh, Pod...' said Homily and began again to tremble. The thought of living in a badger's set had been bad enough, but the thought of not having even that to go to seemed almost worse. 'And I dare say I could have got it nice in the end,' she said, 'providing we lived quite separate—'

'Well, it's no good thinking of it now,' said Pod. He turned to Arrietty: 'What does your Uncle Hendreary say in his letter?'

'Yes,' exclaimed Homily, 'where's this letter?'

'It doesn't say much,' said Arrietty, passing over the paper; 'it just says "Tell your Aunt Lupy to come home".'

'What?' exclaimed Homily sharply, looking at the letter upside-down. 'Come home? What can he mean?'

'He means,' said Pod, 'that Lupy must have set off to come here and that she never arrived.'

'Set off to come here?' repeated Homily. 'But when?'

'How should I know?' said Pod.

'It doesn't say when,' said Arrietty.

'But,' exclaimed Homily, 'it might have been weeks ago!'

'It might,' said Pod. 'Long enough anyway for him to want her back.'

'Oh,' cried Homily, 'all those poor little children!'

'They're growing up now,' said Pod.

'But something must have happened to her!' exclaimed Homily.

'Yes,' said Pod. He turned to Arrietty. 'See what I mean, Arrietty, about those fields?'

'Oh, Pod,' said Homily, her eyes full of tears. 'I don't suppose none of us'll ever see poor Lupy again!'

'Well, we wouldn't have anyway,' said Pod.

'Pod,' said Homily soberly, 'I'm frightened. Everything

seems to be happening at once. What are we going to do?'

'Well,' said Pod, 'there's nothing we can do tonight. That's certain. But have a bit of supper and a good night's rest.' He rose to his feet.

'Oh, Arrietty,' wailed Homily suddenly, 'you naughty, wicked girl! How could you go and start all this? How could you go and talk to a human bean? If only——'

'I was "seen",' cried Arrietty. 'I couldn't help being "seen". Papa was "seen". I don't think it's all as awful as you're trying to make out. I don't think human beans are all that bad——'

'They're bad and they're good,' said Pod; 'they're honest and they're artful——it's just as it takes them at the moment. And animals, if they could talk, would say the same. Steer clear of them——that's what I've always been told. No matter what they promise you. No good never really came to no one from any human bean.'

CHAPTER FIFTEEN

That night, while Arrietty lay straight and still under her cigar-box ceiling, Homily and Pod talked for hours. They talked in the sitting-room, they talked in the kitchen, and later, much later, she heard them talk in their bedroom. She heard drawers shutting and opening, doors creaking, and boxes being pulled out from under beds. 'What are they doing?' she wondered. 'What will happen next?' Very still she lay in her soft little bed with her familiar belongings about her: her postage stamp view of Rio harbour; her silver pig off a charm bracelet; her turquoise ring which sometimes, for fun, she would wear as a crown, and, dearest of all, her floating ladies with the golden trumpets, tooting above their peaceful town. She did not want to lose these, she realized suddenly, lying there straight and still in bed, but to have all the other things as well, adventure and safety mixed—that's what she wanted. And that (the restless hangings and whisperings told her) is just what you couldn't do.

As it happened, Homily was only fidgeting: opening drawers and shutting them, unable to be still. And she ended up, when Pod was already in bed, by deciding to curl her hair. 'Now, Homily,' Pod protested wearily, lying there in his nightshirt, 'there's really no call for that. Who's going to see you?'

'That's just it,' exclaimed Homily, searching in a drawer for her curl-rags; 'in times like these one never knows. I'm not going to be caught out,' she said irritably, turning the drawer upside down and picking over the spilled contents, 'with me hair like this!'

She came to bed at last, looking spiky, like a washed-out golliwog, and Pod with a sigh turned over at last and closed his eyes.

Homily lay for a long time staring at the oil-lamp; it was the silver cap of a scent-bottle with a tiny, floating wick. She felt unwilling, for some reason, to blow it out. There were movements upstairs in the kitchen above and it was late for movements—the household should be asleep and the lumpy curlers pressed uncomfortably against her neck. She gazed— just as Arrietty had done—about the familiar room (too full, she realized, with little bags and boxes and make-shift cupboards) and thought: 'What now? Perhaps nothing will happen after all; the child perhaps is right, and we are making a good deal of fuss about nothing very much; this boy, when all's said and done, is only a guest; perhaps,' thought Homily, 'he'll go away again quite soon, and that,' she told herself drowsily, 'will be that.'

Later (as she realized afterwards) she must have dozed off because it seemed she was crossing Parkin's Beck; it was night and the wind was blowing and the field seemed very steep; she was scrambling up it, along the ridge by the gas-pipe, sliding and falling in the wet grass. The trees, it seemed to Homily, were threshing and clashing, their branches waving and sawing against the sky. Then (as she told them many weeks later) there was a sound of splintering wood...

And Homily woke up. She saw the room again and the oil-lamp flickering, but something, she knew at once, was different: there was a strange draught and her mouth felt dry and full of grit. Then she looked up at the ceiling: Pod!' she shrieked, clutching his shoulder.

Pod rolled over and sat up. They both stared at the ceiling: the whole surface was on a steep slant and one side of it had come right away from the wall—this was what had caused the draught—and down into the room, to within an inch of the foot of the bed, protruded a curious object: a huge bar of grey steel with a flattened, shining edge.

'It's a screwdriver,' said Pod.

They stared at it, fascinated, unable to move, and for a moment all was still. Then slowly the huge object swayed upwards until the sharp edge lay against their ceiling and Homily heard a scrape on the floor above and a sudden human gasp. 'Oh, my knees,' cried Homily, 'oh, my feeling' as, with a splintering wrench, their whole roof flew off and fell down with a clatter, somewhere out of sight.

Homily screamed then. But this time it was a real scream, loud and shrill and hearty; she seemed almost to settle down in her scream, while her eyes stared up, half interested, into empty lighted space. There was another ceiling, she realized, away up above them—higher, it seemed, than the sky; a ham hung from it and two strings of onions. Arrietty appeared in the doorway, scared and trembling, clutching her night-gown. And Pod slapped Homily's back. 'Have done,' he said, 'that's enough,' and Homily, suddenly, was quiet.

A great face appeared then between them and that distant height. It wavered above them, smiling and terrible: there was silence and Homily sat bolt upright, her mouth open. 'Is that your mother?' asked a surprised voice after a moment, and Arrietty from the doorway whispered: 'Yes.'

It was the boy.

Pod got out of bed and stood beside it, shivering in his night-shirt. 'Come on,' he said to Homily, 'you can't stay there!'

But Homily could. She had her old night-dress on with the patch in the back and nothing was going to move her. A slow anger was rising up in Homily: she had been caught in her hair-curlers; Pod had raised his hand to her; and she remembered that, in the general turmoil and for once in her life, she had left the supper washing-up for morning, and there it would be, on the kitchen table, for all the world to see!

She glared at the boy—he was only a child after all. 'Put it back!' she said, 'put it back at once!' Her eyes flashed and her curlers seemed to quiver.

He knelt down then, but Homily did not flinch as the great face came slowly closer. She saw his under-lip, pink and full—like an enormous exaggeration of Arrietty's—and she saw it wobble slightly. 'But I've got something for you,' he said.

Homily's expression did not change, and Arrietty called out from her place in the doorway: 'What have you got?'

The boy reached behind him and very gingerly, careful to keep it upright, he held a wooden object above their heads. 'It's this,' he said, and carefully, his tongue out and breathing heavily, he lowered the object slowly into their hole: it was a doll's dresser, complete with plates. It had two drawers in it and a cupboard below; he adjusted its position at the foot of Homily's bed. Arrietty ran round to see better.

'Oh,' she cried ecstatically. 'Mother, look!'

Homily threw the dresser a glance—it was dark oak and the plates were hand-painted and then she looked quickly away again. 'Yes,' she said coldly, 'it's very nice.'

There was a short silence which no one knew how to break.

'The cupboard really opens,' said the boy at last, and the great hand came down all amongst them, smelling of bath soap. Arrietty flattened herself against the wall and Pod exclaimed, nervous: 'Now then!'

'Yes,' agreed Homily after a moment, 'I see it does.'

Pod drew a long breath—a sigh of relief as the hand went back.

'There, Homily,' he said placatingly, 'you've always wanted something like that!'

'Yes,' said Homily—she still sat bolt upright, her hands clasped in her lap. 'Thank you very much. And now,' she went on coldly, 'will you please put back the roof?'

'Wait a minute,' pleaded the boy. Again he reached behind him; again the hand came down; and there, beside the dresser, where there was barely room for it, was a very small doll's chair; it was a Victorian chair, upholstered in red velvet. 'Oh!' Arrietty exclaimed again and Pod said shyly: 'Just about fit me, that would.'

'Try it,' begged the boy, and Pod threw him a nervous glance. 'Go on!' said Arrietty, and Pod sat down—in his night-shirt, his bare feet showing. 'That's nice,' he said after a moment.

'It would go by the fire in the sitting-room,' cried Arrietty; 'it would look lovely on red blotting-paper!'

'Let's try it,' said the boy, and the hand came down again. Pod sprang up just in time to steady the dresser as the red velvet chair was whisked away above his head and placed presumably in the next room but one. Arrietty ran out of the door and along the passage to see. 'Oh,' she called out to her parents, 'come and see. It's lovely!'

But Pod and Homily did not move. The boy was leaning over them, breathing hard, and they could see the middle buttons of his night-shirt. He seemed to be examining the farther room.

'What do you keep in that mustard-pot?' he asked.

'Coal,' said Arrietty's voice. 'And I helped to borrow this new carpet. Here's the watch I told you about, and the pictures…'

'I could get you some better stamps than those,' the boy said. 'I've got some jubilee ones with the Taj Mahal.'

'Look,' cried Arrietty's voice again, and Pod took Homily's hand, 'these are my books—'

Homily clutched Pod as the great hand came down once more in the direction of Arrietty. 'Quiet,' he whispered; 'sit still...' The boy, it seemed, was touching the books.

'What are they called?' he asked, and Arrietty reeled off the names.

'Pod,' whispered Homily, 'I'm going to scream—'

'No,' whispered Pod. 'You mustn't. Not again.'

'I feel it coming on,' said Homily.

Pod looked worried. 'Hold your breath,' he said, 'and count ten.'

The boy was saying to Arrietty: 'Why couldn't you read me those?'

'Well, I could,' said Arrietty, 'but I'd rather read something new.'

'But you never come,' complained the boy.

'I know,' said Arrietty, 'but I will.'

'Pod,' whispered Homily, 'did you hear that? Did you hear what she said?'

'Yes, yes,' Pod whispered; 'keep quiet—'

'Do you want to see the store-rooms?' Arrietty suggested next and Homily clapped a hand to her mouth as though to stifle a cry.

Pod looked up at the boy. 'Hey,' he called, trying to attract his attention. The boy looked down. 'Put the roof back now,' Pod begged him, trying to sound matter of fact and reasonable; 'we're getting cold.'

'All right,' agreed the boy, but he seemed to hesitate: he reached across them for the piece of board which formed their roof. 'Shall I nail you down?' he asked, and they saw him pick up the hammer; it swayed above them, very dangerous-looking.

'Of course nail us down,' said Pod irritably.

'I mean,' said the boy, 'I've got some more things upstairs—'

Pod looked uncertain and Homily nudged him. 'Ask him,' she whispered, 'what kind of things?'

'What kind of things?' asked Pod.

'Things from an old doll's house there is on the top shelf of the cupboard by the fire-place in the schoolroom.'

'I've never seen no doll's house,' said Pod.

'Well, it's in the cupboard,' said the boy, 'right up by the ceiling; you can't see it—you've got to climb on the lower shelves to get to it.'

'What sort of things *are* there in the doll's house?' asked Arrietty from the sitting-room.

'Oh, everything,' the boy told her; 'carpets and rugs and beds with mattresses, and there's a bird in a cage—not a real one, of course—and cooking pans and tables, and five gilt chairs and a pot with a palm in it—a dish of plaster tarts and an imitation leg of mutton—'

Homily leaned across to Pod. 'Tell him to nail us down lightly,' she whispered. Pod stared at her and she nodded vigorously, clasping her hands.

Pod turned to the boy. 'All right,' he said, 'you nail us down. But lightly, if you see what I mean. Just a tap or two here and there...'

CHAPTER SIXTEEN

Then began a curious phase in their lives: borrowings beyond all dreams of borrowing—a golden age. Every night the floor was opened and treasures would appear: a real carpet for the sitting-room, a tiny coalscuttle, a stiff little sofa with damask cushions, a double bed with a round bolster, a single ditto with a striped mattress, framed pictures instead of stamps, a kitchen stove which didn't work, but which looked 'lovely' in the kitchen; there were oval tables and square tables and a little desk with one drawer; there were two maple wardrobes (one with a looking-glass) and a bureau with curved legs. Homily grew not only accustomed to the roof coming off but even went so far as to suggest to Pod that he put the board on hinges. 'It's just the hammering, I don't care for,' she explained; 'it brings down the dirt.'

When the boy brought them a grand piano Homily begged Pod to build a drawing-room. 'Next to the sitting-room,' she said, 'and we could move the store-rooms farther down. Then we could have those gilt chairs he talks about and the palm in a pot...' Pod, however, was a little tired of furniture removing; he was looking forward to the quiet evenings when he could doze at last beside the fire in his new velvet chair. No sooner had he put a chest of drawers in one place when

Homily, coming in and out of the door—'to get the effect'—
made him 'try' it somewhere else. And every evening, at
about his usual bedtime, the roof would fly up and more stuff
would arrive. But Homily was tireless; bright-eyed and pink-
cheeked, after a long day's pushing and pulling, she still
would leave nothing until morning. 'Let's just *try* it,' she
would beg, lifting up one end of a large doll's side-board, so
that Pod would have to lift the other; 'it won't take a minute!'
But as Pod well knew, in actual fact it would be several hours
before, dishevelled and aching, they finally dropped into bed.
Even then Homily would sometimes hop out 'to have one last
look'.

In the meantime, in payment for these riches, Arrietty
would read to the boy—every afternoon in the long grass
beyond the cherry-tree. He would lie on his back and she
would stand beside his shoulder and tell him when to turn the
page. They were happy days to look back on afterwards, with
the blue sky beyond the cherry boughs, the grasses softly stir-
ring, and the boy's great ear listening beside her. She grew to
know that ear quite well, with its curves and shadows and
sunlit pinks and golds. Sometimes, as she grew bolder, she
would lean against his shoulder. He was very still while she
read to him and always grateful. What worlds they would
explore together—strange worlds to Arrietty. She learned a
lot and some of the things she learned were hard to accept.
She was made to realize once and for all that this earth on
which they lived turning about in space did not revolve, as

she had believed, for the sake of little people, 'Nor for big people either,' she reminded the boy when she saw his secret smile.

In the cool of the evening Pod would come for her—a rather weary Pod, dishevelled and dusty—to take her back for tea. And at home there would be an excited Homily and fresh delights to discover. 'Shut your eyes!' Homily would cry. 'Now open them!' and Arrietty, in a dream of joy, would see her home transformed. All kinds of surprises there were—even, one day, lace curtains at the grating, looped up with pink string.

Their only sadness was that there was no one there to see: no visitors, no casual droppers-in, no admiring cries and envious glances! What would Homily have not given for an Overmantel or a Harpsichord? Even a Rain-Barrel would have been better than no one at all. 'You write to your Uncle Hendreary,' Homily suggested, 'and tell *him*. A nice long letter, mind, and don't leave anything out!' Arrietty began the letter on the back of one of the discarded pieces of blotting-paper, but it became as she wrote it just a dull list, far too long, like a sale catalogue or the inventory of a house to let; she would have to keep jumping up to count spoons or to look up words in the dictionary, and after a while she laid it aside: there was so much else to do, so many new books to read, and so much, now, that she could talk of with the boy.

'He's been ill,' she told her mother and father; 'he's been here for the quiet and the country air. But soon he'll go back to India. Did you know,' she asked the amazed Homily, 'that the Arctic night lasts six months, and that the distance between the two poles is less than that between the two extremities of a diameter drawn through the equator?'

Yes, they were happy days and all would have been well, as Pod said afterwards, if they had stuck to borrowing from the doll's house. No one in the human household seemed to remember it was there and, consequently, nothing was missed. The drawing-room, however, could not help but be a temptation: it was so seldom used nowadays; there were so many knick-knack tables which had been out of Pod's reach, and the boy, of course, could turn the key in the glass doors of the cabinet.

The silver violin he brought them first and then the silver harp; it stood no higher than Pod's shoulder and Pod restrung it with horse-hair from the sofa in the morning-room. 'A musical conversazione, that's what we could have!' cried the exulting Homily as Arrietty struck a tiny, tuneless note on a horse-hair string. 'If only,' she went on fervently, clasping her hands, 'your father would start on the drawing-room!' (She curled her hair nearly every evening nowadays and, since the house was more or less straight, she would occasionally change for dinner into a satin dress; it hung like a sack, but Homily called it 'Grecian'.) 'We could use your painted ceiling,' she explained to Arrietty, 'and there are quite enough of those toy builders' bricks to make a parquet floor.' ('Parkay,' she would say, 'Par-r-r-kay...' just like a Harpsichord.) Even

Great Aunt Sophy, right away upstairs in the littered grandeur of her bedroom, seemed distantly affected by a spirit of endeavour which seemed to flow, in gleeful whorls and eddies, about the staid old house. Several times lately Pod, when he went to her room, had found her out of bed. He went there nowadays not to borrow, but to rest: the room, one might almost say, had become his club; a place to which he could go 'to get away from things'. Pod was a little irked by his riches; he had never visualized, not in his wildest dreams, borrowing such as this. Homily, he felt, should call a halt; surely, now, their home was grand enough; these jewelled snuff-boxes and diamond encrusted miniatures, these filigree vanity-cases and Dresden figurines—all, as he knew, from the drawing-room cabinet—were not really necessary: what was the good of a shepherdess nearly as tall as Arrietty or an outsize candle-snuffer? Sitting just inside the fender, where he could warm his hands at the fire, he watched Aunt Sophy hobble slowly round the room on her two sticks. 'She'll be downstairs soon, I shouldn't wonder,' he thought glumly, hardly listening to her oft-told tale about a royal luncheon aboard a Russian yacht, 'then she'll miss these things...'

It was not Aunt Sophy, however, who missed them first. It was Mrs Driver. Mrs Driver had never forgotten the trouble over Rosa Pickhatchet. It had not been, at the time, easy to pin-point the guilt. Even Crampfurl had felt under suspicion. 'From now on,' Mrs Driver had said, 'I'll manage on me own. No more strange maids in *this* house!' A drop of Madeira here, a pair of old stockings there, a handkerchief or so, an odd vest, or an occasional pair of gloves—these, Mrs Driver felt, were different; these were within her rights. But trinkets out of the drawing-room cabinet that, she told herself grimly, staring at the depleted shelves, was a different story altogether!

Standing there, on that fateful day, in the spring sunshine, feather duster in hand, her little black eyes had become slits of anger and cunning. She felt tricked. It was, she calculated, as though someone, suspecting her dishonesty, were trying to catch her out. But who could it be? Crampfurl? That boy? The man who came to wind the clocks? These things had disappeared gradually, one by one: it was someone, of that she felt sure, who knew the house—and someone who wished her ill. Could it, she wondered suddenly, be the mistress herself? The old girl had been out of bed lately and walking about her room. Might she not have come downstairs in the night, poking about with her stick, snooping and spying (Mrs Driver remembered suddenly the empty Madeira bottle and the two glasses which, so often, were left on the kitchen table). 'Ah,' thought Mrs Driver, 'was not this just the sort of thing she might do—the sort of thing she would cackle over, back upstairs again among her pillows, watching and waiting for Mrs Driver to report the loss?'

'Everything all right downstairs, Driver?' that's what she'd always say and she would look at Mrs Driver sideways out of those mocking old eyes of hers. 'I wouldn't put it past her!'

Mrs Driver exclaimed aloud, gripping her feather duster as though it were a club. 'And a nice merry-andrew she'd look if I caught her at it—creeping about the downstairs rooms in the middle of the night. All right, my lady,' muttered Mrs Driver grimly, 'pry and potter all you want—two can play at that game!'

CHAPTER SEVENTEEN

Mrs Driver was short with Crampfurl that evening; she would not sit down and drink with him as usual, but stumped about the kitchen, looking at him sideways every now and again out of the corners of her eyes. He looked uneasy—as indeed he was: there was a kind of menace in her silence, a hidden something which no one could ignore. Even Aunt Sophy had felt it when Mrs Driver brought up her wine; she heard it in the clink of the decanter against the glass as Mrs Driver set down the tray and in the rattle of the wooden rings as Mrs Driver drew the curtains; it was in the tremble of the floorboards as Mrs Driver crossed the room and in the click of the latch as Mrs Driver closed the door. 'What's the matter with her now?' Aunt Sophy wondered vaguely as delicately, ungreedily, she poured the first glass.

The boy had felt it too. From the way Mrs Driver had stared at him as he sat hunched in the bath; from the way she soaped the loofah and the way she said: 'And now!' She had scrubbed him slowly, with a careful, angry steadiness, and all through the bathing time she did not say a word. When he was in bed she had gone through all his things, peering into cupboards and opening his drawers. She had pulled his suitcase out from under the wardrobe and found his dear dead mole and his hoard of sugar-lumps and her best potato knife. But even then she had not spoken. She had thrown the mole into the waste paper basket and had made sharp noises with her tongue; she pocketed the potato knife and all the sugar-lumps. She had stared at him a moment before she turned the gas low—a strange stare it had been, more puzzled than accusing.

Mrs Driver slept above the scullery. She had her own back-stairs. That night she did not undress. She set the alarm clock for midnight and put it, where the tick would not disturb her, outside her door; she unbuttoned her tight shoes and crawled, grunting a little, under the eiderdown. She had 'barely closed her eyes' (as she told Crampfurl afterwards) when the clock shrilled off—chattering and rattling on its four thin legs on the bare boards of the passage-way. Mrs Driver tumbled herself out of bed and fumbled her way to the door. 'Shush,' she said to the clock as she felt for the catch. 'Shush!' and clasped it to her bosom. She stood there, in her stockinged feet, at the head of the scullery stairs: something, it seemed, had flickered below—a hint of light. Mrs Driver peered down the dark curve of the narrow stairway. Yes, there it was again—a moth-wing flutter! Candlelight—that's what it was! A moving candle—beyond the stairs, beyond the scullery, somewhere within the kitchen.

Clock in hand, Mrs Driver creaked down the stairs in her stockinged feet, panting a little in her eagerness. There seemed a sigh in the darkness, an echo of movement. And it seemed to Mrs Driver, standing there on the cold stone flags of the scullery, that this sound that was barely a sound could only mean one thing; the soft swing-to of the green baize door—that door which led out of the kitchen into the main hall beyond. Hurriedly Mrs Driver felt her way into the kitchen and fumbled for matches along the ledge above the stove; she knocked off a pepper-pot and a paper bag of cloves, and glancing quickly downwards saw a filament of light; she saw it in the second before she struck a match—a glow-worm thread, it looked like, on the floor beside her feet; it ran in an oblong shape, outlining a rough square. Mrs Driver gasped and lit the gas and the room leapt up around her: she glanced quickly at the baize door; there seemed to her startled eye a quiver of movement in it, as though it had just swung to; she ran to it and pushed it open, but the passage beyond was still and dark—no flicker of shadow nor sound of distant footfall. She let the door fall to again and watched it as it swung back, slowly, regretfully, held by its heavy spring. Yes, that was the sound she had heard from the scullery—that sighing whisper—like an indrawn breath.

Cautiously, clutching back her skirts, Mrs Driver moved towards the stove. An object lay there, something pinkish, on the floor beside the jutting board. Ah, she realized, that board—that was where the light had come from! Mrs Driver hesitated and glanced about the kitchen: everything else looked normal and just as she had left it—the plates on the dresser, the saucepans on the wall, and the row of tea-towels hanging symmetrically on their string above the stove. The pinkish object, she saw now, was a heart-shaped-cachou-box—one that she knew well—from the glassed-in tray-table beside the fire-place in the drawing-room. She picked it up; it was enamel and gold and set with tiny brilliants. 'Well, I'm—' she began, and stooping swiftly with a sudden angry movement, she wrenched back the piece of floor.

And then she shrieked, loud and long. She saw movement: a running, a scrambling, a fluttering! She heard a squeaking, a jabbering, and a gasping. Little people, they looked like, with hands and feet... and mouths opening.

That's what they looked like... but they couldn't *be* that, of course! Running here, there, and everywhere. 'Oh! oh! oh!' she shrieked and felt behind her for a chair. She clambered on to it and it wobbled beneath her and she climbed, still shrieking, from the chair to the table.

And there she stood, marooned, crying and gasping, and calling out for help, until, after hours it seemed, there was a rattling at the scullery door. Crampfurl it was, roused at last by the light and the noise. 'What is it?' he called. 'Let me in!' But Mrs Driver would not leave the table. 'A nest! A nest!' she shouted. 'Alive and squeaking!'

Crampfurl threw his weight against the door and burst open the lock. He staggered, slightly dazed, into the kitchen, his corduroy trousers pulled on over his night-shirt. 'Where?' he cried, his eyes wide beneath his tousled hair. 'What sort of a nest?'

Mrs Driver, sobbing still with fright, pointed at the floor. Crampfurl walked over in his slow, deliberate way and stared down. He saw a hole in the floor, lined and cluttered with small objects—children's toys, they looked like, bits of rubbish that was all. 'It's nothing,' he said after a moment; 'it's that boy, that's what it is.' He stirred the contents with his foot and all the partitions fell down. 'There ain't nothing alive in there.'

'But I saw them, I tell you,' gasped Mrs Driver, 'little people—like with hands—or mice dressed up...'

Crampfurl stared into the hole. 'Mice dressed up?' he repeated uncertainly.

'Hundreds of them,' went on Mrs Driver, 'running and squeaking. I saw them, I tell you!'

'Well, there ain't nothing there now,' said Crampfurl and he gave a final stir round with his boot.

'Then they've run away,' she cried, 'under the floor... up inside the walls... the place is alive with them.'

'Well,' said Crampfurl stolidly, 'maybe. But if you ask me, I think it's that boy—where he hides things.' His eye brightened and he went down on one knee. 'Where he's got the ferret, I shouldn't wonder.'

'Listen,' cried Mrs Driver, and there was a despairing note in her voice, 'you've got to listen. This wasn't no boy and it wasn't no ferret.' She reached for the back of the chair and lowered herself clumsily on to the floor; she came beside him to the edge of the hole. 'They had hands and faces, I tell you.

Look,' she said, pointing, 'see that? It's a bed. And now I come to think of it one of 'em was in it.'

'Now you come to think of it,' said Crampfurl.

'Yes,' went on Mrs Driver firmly, 'and there's something else I come to think of. Remember that girl, Rosa Pickhatchet?'

'The one that was simple?'

'Well, simple or not, she saw one—on the drawing-room mantelpiece, with a beard.'

'One what?' asked Crampfurl.

Mrs Driver glared at him. 'What I've been telling you about—one of these—these—'

'Mice dressed up?' said Crampfurl.

'Not mice!' Mrs Driver almost shouted. 'Mice don't have beards.'

'But you said—' began Crampfurl.

'Yes, I know I said it. Not that these had beards. But what would you call them? What could they be but mice?'

'Not so loud!' whispered Crampfurl. 'You'll wake the house up.'

'They can't hear,' said Mrs Driver, 'not through the baize door.' She went to the stove and picked up the fire-tongs. 'And what if they do? We ain't done nothing. Move over,' she went on, 'and let me get at the hole.'

One by one Mrs Driver picked things out—with many shocked gasps, cries of amazement, and did-you-evers. She made two piles on the floor—one of valuables and one of what she called 'rubbish'. Curious objects dangled from the tongs: 'Would you believe it—her best lace handkerchiefs! Look, here's another... and another! And my big mattress needle—I knew I had one—my silver thimble, if you please, and one of hers! And look, oh my, at the wools... the cottons! No wonder you can never find a reel of white cotton if you want one. Potatoes... nuts... look at this, a pot of caviare... CAVIARE! No, it's too much, it really is. Doll's chairs... tables.... and look at all this blotting-paper—so that's where it goes! Oh, my goodness gracious!' she cried suddenly, her eyes staring. 'What's this?' Mrs Driver laid down the tongs and leaned over the hole tentatively and fearfully as though afraid of being stung. 'It's a watch—an emerald watch—her watch! And she's never missed it!' Her voice rose. 'And it's going! Look, you can see by the kitchen clock! Twenty-five past twelve!' Mrs Driver sat down suddenly on a hard chair; her eyes were staring and her face looked white and flabby, as though deflated. 'You know what this means?' she said to Crampfurl.

'No?' he said.

'The police,' said Mrs Driver, 'that's what this means—a case for the police.'

CHAPTER EIGHTEEN

The boy lay, trembling a little, beneath the bedclothes. The screwdriver was under his mattress. He had heard the alarm clock; he had heard Mrs Driver exclaim on the stairs and he had run. The candle on the table beside his bed still smelt a little and the wax must still be warm. He lay there waiting, but they did not come upstairs. After hours, it seemed, he heard the hall clock strike one. All seemed quiet below, and at last he slipped out of bed and crept along the passage to the head of the stairway. There he sat for a while, shivering a little, and gazing downwards into the darkened hall. There was no sound but the steady tick of the clock and occasionally that shuffle or whisper which might be wind, but which, as he knew, was the sound of the house itself—the sigh of the tired floors and the ache of knotted wood. So quiet it was that at last he found courage to move and to tiptoe down the staircase and along the kitchen passage. He listened awhile outside the baize door, and at length, very gently, he pushed it open. The kitchen was silent and filled with greyish darkness. He felt, as Mrs Driver had done, along the shelf for the matches and he struck a light. He saw the gaping hole in the floor and the objects piled beside it and, in the same flash, he saw a candle on the shelf. He lit it clumsily, with trembling hands. Yes, there they lay—the contents of the little home—higgledy-piggledy on the boards and the tongs lay beside them. Mrs Driver had carried away all she considered valuable and had left the 'rubbish'. And rubbish it looked thrown down like this—balls of wool, old potatoes, odd pieces of doll's furniture, match-boxes, cotton-reels, crumpled squares of blotting-paper...

He knelt down. The 'house' itself was a shambles—partitions fallen, earth floors revealed (where Pod had dug down to give greater height to the rooms), match-sticks, an old cogwheel, onion-skins, scattered bottle-tops... The boy stared, blinking his eyelids and tilting the candle so that the grease ran hot on his hand. Then he got up from his knees and, crossing the kitchen on tiptoe, he closed the scullery door. He came back to the hole and, leaning down, he called softly: 'Arrietty... Arrietty!' After a while he called again. Something else fell hot on his hand: it was a tear from his eye. Angrily he brushed it away, and, leaning farther into the hole, he called once more. 'Pod,' he whispered. 'Homily!'

They appeared so quietly that at first, in the wavering light of the candle, he did not see them. Silent they stood, looking up at him with scared white faces from what had been the passage outside the store-rooms.

'Where have you been?' asked the boy.

Pod cleared his throat. 'Up at the end of the passage. Under the clock.'

'I've got to get you out,' said the boy.

'Where to?' asked Pod.

'I don't know. What about the attic?'

'That ain't no good,' said Pod. 'I heard them talking. They're going to get the police and a cat and the sanitary inspector and the rat-catcher from the town hall at Leighton Buzzard.'

They were all silent. Little eyes stared at big eyes. 'There won't be nowhere in the house that's safe,' Pod said at last. And no one moved.

'What about the doll's house on the top shelf in the schoolroom?' suggested the boy. 'Even a cat can't get there.'

Homily gave a little moan of assent. 'Yes,' she said, 'the doll's house...'

'No,' said Pod in the same expressionless voice, 'you can't live on a shelf. Maybe the cat can't get up, but no more can't you get down. You're stuck. You got to have water.'

'I'd bring you water,' said the boy; he touched the pile of 'rubbish'. 'And there are beds and things here.'

'No,' said Pod, 'a shelf ain't no good. Besides, you'll be going soon, or so they say.'

'Oh, Pod,' pleaded Homily in a husky whisper, 'there's stairs in the doll's house, and two bedrooms, and a dining room, and a kitchen. And a bathroom!' she said.

'But it's up by the ceiling,' Pod explained wearily. 'You got to eat, haven't you,' he asked, 'and drink?'

'Yes, Pod, I know. But—'

'There ain't no buts,' said Pod. He drew a long breath. 'We

got to emigrate,' he said.

'Oh,' moaned Homily softly and Arrietty began to cry.

'Now don't take on,' said Pod in a tired voice.

Arrietty had covered her face with her hands and her tears ran through her fingers; the boy, watching, saw them glisten in the candlelight. 'I'm not taking on,' she gasped. 'I'm so happy... happy.'

'You mean,' said the boy to Pod, but with one eye on Arrietty, 'you'll go to the badger's set?' He too felt a mounting excitement.

'Where else?' asked Pod.

'Oh, my goodness gracious!' moaned Homily, and sat down on the broken match-box chest of drawers.

'But you've got to go somewhere tonight,' said the boy. 'You've got to go somewhere before tomorrow morning.'

'Oh, my goodness gracious!' moaned Homily again.

'He's right at that,' said Pod. 'Can't cross them fields in the dark. Bad enough getting across them in daylight.'

'I know,' cried Arrietty. Her wet face glistened in the candlelight; it was alight and tremulous and she raised her arms a little as though about to fly, and she swayed as she balanced on her toe-tips. 'Let's go to the doll's house just for tonight and tomorrow'—she closed her eyes against the brightness of the vision—'tomorrow the boy will take us—take us—' and she could not say to where.

'Take us?' cried Homily in a strange hollow voice. 'How?'

'In his pockets,' chanted Arrietty; 'won't you?' Again she swayed, with lighted upturned face.

'Yes,' he said, 'and bring the luggage up afterwards—in a fish basket.'

'Oh, my goodness!' moaned Homily.

'I'll pick all the furniture out of this pile here. Or most of it. They'll hardly notice. And anything else you want.'

'Tea,' murmured Homily. 'Enough for our lifetimes.'

'All right,' said the boy. 'I'll get a pound of tea. And coffee too if you like. And cooking pots. And matches. You'll be all right,' he said.

'But what do they eat?' wailed Homily. 'Caterpillars?'

'Now, Homily,' said Pod, 'don't be foolish. Lupy was always a good manager.'

'But Lupy isn't there,' said Homily. 'Berries. Do they eat berries? How do they cook? Out of doors?'

'Now, Homily,' said Pod, 'we'll see all that when we get there.'

'I couldn't light a fire of sticks,' said Homily, 'not in the wind. What if it rains?' she asked. 'How do they cook in the rain?'

'Now, Homily—' began Pod—he was beginning to lose patience—but Homily rushed on.

'Could you get us a couple of tins of sardines to take?' she asked the boy. 'And some salt? And some candles? And matches? And could you bring us the carpets from the doll's house?'

'Yes,' said the boy, 'I could. Of course I could. Anything you want.'

'All right,' said Homily. She still looked wild, partly because some of her hair had rolled out of the curlers, but she seemed appeased. 'How are you going to get us upstairs? Up to the schoolroom?'

The boy looked down at his pocketless night-shirt. 'I'll carry you,' he said.

'How?' asked Homily. 'In your hands?'

'Yes,' said the boy.

'I'd rather die,' said Homily. 'I'd rather stay right here and be eaten by the rat-catcher from the town hall at Leighton Buzzard.'

The boy looked round the kitchen; he seemed bewildered. 'Shall I carry you in the peg-bag?' he asked at last, seeing it hanging in its usual place on the handle of the scullery door.

'All right,' said Homily. 'Take out the pegs first.'

But she walked into it bravely enough when he laid it out on the floor. It was soft and floppy and made of woven raffia. When he picked it up Homily shrieked and clung to Pod and Arrietty. 'Oh,' she gasped as the bag swayed a little, 'oh, I can't! Stop it! Put me out! Oh! Oh!' And, clutching and slipping, they fell into a tangle at the bottom.

'Be quiet, Homily, can't you!' exclaimed Pod angrily, and held her tightly by the ankle. It was not easy to control her as he was lying on his back with his face pushed forward on his chest and one leg, held upright by the side of the bag, somewhere above his head. Arrietty climbed up, away from them, clinging to the knots of raffia, and looked out over the edge.

'Oh, I can't! I can't!' cried Homily. 'Stop it, Pod. I'm dying. Tell him to put us down.'

'Put us down,' said Pod in his patient way, 'just for a moment. That's right. On the floor,' and, as once again the bag was placed beside the hole, they all ran out.

'Look here,' said the boy unhappily to Homily, 'you've got to try.'

'She'll try all right,' said Pod. 'Give her a breather, and take it slower, if you see what I mean.'

'All right,' agreed the boy, 'but there isn't much time. Come on,' he said nervously, 'hop in.'

'Listen!' cried Pod sharply, and froze.

The boy, looking down, saw their three upturned faces catching the light—like pebbles they looked, still and stony, against the darkness within the hole. And then in a flash they were gone—the boards were empty and the hole was bare. He leaned into it. 'Pod!' he called in a frantic whisper. 'Homily! Come back!' And then he too became frozen, stooped and rigid above the hole. The scullery door creaked open behind him.

It was Mrs Driver. She stood there silent, this time in her night-dress. Turning, the boy stared up at her. 'Hallo,' he said, uncertainly, after a moment.

She did not smile, but something lightened in her eyes— a malicious gleam, a look of triumph. She carried a candle which shone upwards on her face, streaking it strangely with light and shadow. 'What are you doing down here?' she asked.

He stared at her, but he did not speak.

'Answer me,' she said. 'And what are you doing with the peg-bag?'

Still he stared at her, almost stupidly. 'The peg-bag?' he repeated and looked down as though surprised to see it in his hand.

'Nothing,' he said.

'Was it you who put the watch in the hole?'

'No,' he said, staring up at her again, 'it was there already.'

'Ah,' she said and smiled, 'so you knew it was there?'

'No,' he said; 'I mean yes.'

'Do you know what you are?' asked Mrs Driver, watching him closely. 'You are a sneaking, thieving, noxious little dribbet of no-good!'

His face quivered. 'Why?' he said.

'You know why. You're a wicked, blackhearted, fribbling little pickpocket. That's what you are. And, so are they. They're nasty, crafty, scampy, scurvy, squeaking little—'

'No they're not,' he put in quickly.

'And you're in league with them!' She came across to him and, taking him by the upper arm, she jerked him to his feet. 'You know what they do with thieves?' she asked.

'No,' he said.

'They lock them up. That's what they do with thieves. And

that's what's going to happen to you!'

'I'm not a thief,' cried the boy, his lips trembling. 'I'm a Borrower.'

'A what?' She swung him round by tightening the grip on his arm.

'A Borrower,' he repeated; there were tears on his eyelids; he hoped they would not fall.

'So that's what you call it!' she exclaimed (as he himself had done—so long ago, it seemed now—that day with Arrietty).

'That's their name,' he said. 'The kind of people they are—they're Borrowers.'

'Borrowers, eh?' repeated Mrs Driver wonderingly. She laughed. 'Well, they've done all the borrowing they're ever going to do in this house!' She began to drag him towards the door.

The tears spilled over his eyelids and ran down his cheeks. 'Don't hurt them,' he begged. 'I'll move them. I promise. I know how.'

Mrs Driver laughed again and pushed him roughly through the green baize door. 'They'll be moved all right,' she said. 'Don't worry. The rat-catcher will know how. Crampfurl's old cat will know how. So will the sanitary inspector. And the fire brigade, if need be. The police'll know how, I shouldn't wonder. No need to worry about moving them. Once you've found the nest,' she went on, dropping her voice to a vicious whisper as they passed Aunt Sophy's door;

'the rest is easy!'

She pushed him into the schoolroom and locked the door and he heard the boards of the passage creak beneath her tread as, satisfied, she moved away. He crept into bed then, because he was cold, and cried his heart out under the blankets.

CHAPTER NINETEEN

'And that,' said Mrs May, laying down her crochet hook, 'is really the end.'

Kate stared at her. 'Oh, it can't be,' she gasped, 'oh, please... please...'

'The last square,' said Mrs May, smoothing it out on her knee, 'the hundred and fiftieth. Now we can sew them together—'

'Oh,' said Kate, breathing again, 'the quilt! I thought you meant the story.'

'It's the end of the story too,' said Mrs May absently, 'in a way,' and she began to sort out the squares.

'But,' stammered Kate, 'you can't—I mean—' and she looked, quite suddenly, everything they had said she was— wild, self-willed, and all the rest of it. 'It's not fair,' she cried, 'it's cheating. It's—' Tears sprang to her eyes; she threw her work down on the table and darning needle after it, and she kicked the bag of wools which lay beside her on the carpet.

'Why, Kate, why?' Mrs May looked genuinely surprised.

'Something more must have happened,' cried Kate angrily. 'What about the rat-catcher? And the policeman? And the—'

'But something more did happen,' said Mrs May, 'a lot

more happened. I'm going to tell you.'

'Then why did you say it was the end?'

'Because,' said Mrs May (she still looked surprised), 'he never saw them again.'

'Then how can there be more?'

'Because,' said Mrs May, 'there is more.'

Kate glared at her. 'All right,' she said, 'go on.'

Mrs May looked back at her. 'Kate,' she said after a moment, 'stories never really end. They can go on and on and on. It's just that sometimes, at a certain point, one stops telling them.'

'But not at this kind of point,' said Kate.

'Well, thread your needle,' said Mrs May, 'with grey wool, this time. And we'll sew these squares together. I'll start at the top and you can start at the bottom. First a grey square, then an emerald, then a pink, and so on—'

'Then you didn't really mean it,' said Kate irritably, trying to push the folded wool through the narrow eye of the needle, 'when you said he never saw them again?'

'But I did mean it,' said Mrs May. 'I'm telling you just what happened. He had to leave suddenly—at the end of the week—because there was a boat for India and a family who could take him. And for the three days before he left they kept him locked up in those two rooms.'

'For three days!' exclaimed Kate.

'Yes. Mrs Driver, it seemed, told Aunt Sophy that he had a cold. She wasn't unkind to him, but she was determined, you see, to keep him out of the way until she'd got rid of the Borrowers.'

'And did she?' asked Kate. 'I mean—did they all come? The policeman? And the rat-catcher? And the—'

'The sanitary inspector didn't come. At least, not while my brother was there. And they didn't have the rat-catcher from the town hall, but they had the local man. The policeman came—' Mrs May laughed. 'During those three days Mrs Driver used to give my brother a running commentary on what was going on below. She loved to grumble, and my brother, rendered harmless and shut away upstairs, became a kind of neutral. She used to carry his meals up, and, on that first morning, she brought all the doll's furniture up on the breakfast tray and made my brother climb the shelves and put it back in the doll's house. It was then she told him about the policeman. Furious he said she was. He felt almost sorry for her.'

'Why?' asked Kate.

'Because the policeman turned out to be Nellie Runacre's son Ernie, a boy Mrs Driver had chased many a time for stealing russet apples from the tree by the gate—"A nasty, thieving, good-for-nothing dribbet of no good," she told my brother. "Sitting down there he is now, in the kitchen, large as life with his notebook out, laughing fit to bust... twenty-one, he says he is now, and as cheeky as you make 'em..." '

'And was he,' asked Kate, round-eyed, 'a dribbet of no-good?'

'Of course not. Any more than my brother was. Ernie Runacre was a fine, upstanding young man and a credit to the police force. And he did not actually laugh at Mrs Driver when she told him her story, but he gave her what Crampfurl spoke of afterwards as "an old-fashioned look" when she described Homily in bed—"Take more water with it," it seemed to say.'

'More water with what?' asked Kate.

'The Fine Old Pale Madeira, I suppose,' said Mrs May. 'And Great Aunt Sophy had the same suspicion: she was furious when she heard that Mrs Driver had seen several little people when she herself on a full decanter had only risen to one or, at most, two. Crampfurl had to bring all the Madeira up from the cellar and stack the cases against the wall in a corner of Aunt Sophy's bedroom where, as she said, she could keep an eye on it.'

'Did they get a cat?' asked Kate.

'Yes, they did. But that wasn't much of a success either. It was Crampfurl's cat, a large yellow tom with white streaks in it. According to Mrs Driver, it had only two ideas in its head—to get out of the house or into the larder. "Talk of borrowers," Mrs Driver would say as she slammed down the fish-pie for my brother's luncheon, "that cat's a borrower, if ever there was one; borrowed the fish, that cat did, and a good half-bowl of egg sauce!" But the cat wasn't there long. The first thing the rat-catcher's terriers did was to chase it out of the house. There was a dreadful set-to, my brother said.

They chased it everywhere—upstairs and downstairs, in and out all the rooms, barking their heads off. The last glimpse my brother had of the cat was streaking away through the spinney and across the fields with the terriers after it.'

'Did they catch it?'

'No,' Mrs May laughed. 'It was still there when I went, a year later. A little morose, but as fit as a fiddle.'

'Tell about when *you* went.'

'Oh, I wasn't there long,' said Mrs May rather hastily, 'and after that the house was sold. My brother never went back.'

Kate stared at her suspiciously, pressing her needle against the centre of her lower lip. 'So they never caught the little people?' she said at last.

Mrs May's eyes flicked away. 'No, they never actually caught them, but'—she hesitated—'as far as my poor brother was concerned, what they did do seemed even worse.'

'What did they do?'

Mrs May laid down her work and stared for a moment, thoughtfully, at her idle hands. 'I hated the rat-catcher,' she said suddenly.

'Why, did you know him?'

'Everybody knew him. He had a wall eye and his name was Rich William. He was also the pig-killer, and, well—he did other things as well—he had a gun, a hatchet, a spade, a pick-axe, and a contraption with bellows for smoking things out. I don't know what the smoke was exactly—poison fumes of some kind which he made himself from herbs and chemicals. I only remember the smell of it; it clung round the barns or wherever he'd been. You can imagine what my brother felt on that third day, the day he was leaving, when suddenly he smelled that smell.

'He was all dressed and ready to go. The bags were packed and down in the hall. Mrs Driver came and unlocked the door and took him down the passage to Aunt Sophy. He stood there, stiff and pale, in gloves and overcoat beside the curtained bed. "Seasick already?" Aunt Sophy mocked him, peering down at him over the edge of the great mattress.

"No," he said, "it's that smell."

'Aunt Sophy lifted her nose. She sniffed. "What smell is it, Driver?"

"It's the rat-catcher, my lady," explained Mrs Driver, reddening, "down in the kitchen."

"What!" exclaimed Aunt Sophy, "are you smoking them out?" and she began to laugh. "Oh dear... oh dear!" she gasped, "but if you don't like them, Driver, the remedy's simple."

"What is that, my lady?" asked Mrs Driver uncomfortably, and even her chins were red.

'Helpless with laughter Aunt Sophy waved a ringed hand: "Keep the bottle corked," she managed at last and motioned them weakly away. They heard her laughing still as they went on down the stairs.

"She don't believe in them," muttered Mrs Driver, and she tightened her grip on my brother's arm. "More fool her!

She'll change her tune, like enough, when I take them up afterwards, laid out in sizes, on a clean piece of newspaper and she dragged him unceremoniously across the hall.

'The clock had been moved, exposing the wainscot, and, as my brother saw at once, the hole had been blocked and sealed. The front door was open as usual and the sunshine streamed in. The bags stood there beside the fibre mat, cooking a little in the golden warmth. The fruit trees beyond the bank had shed their petals and were lit with tender green, transparent in the sunlight. "Plenty of time," said Mrs Driver, glancing up at the clock, "the cab's not due till three-thirty—" "The clock's stopped," said my brother.

'Mrs Driver turned. She was wearing her hat and her best black coat, ready to take him to the station. She looked strange and tight and chapel-going—not a bit like "Driver". "So it has," she said; her jaw dropped and her cheeks became heavy and pendulous. "It's moving it," she decided after a moment. "It'll be all right," she went on, "once we get it back. Mr Frith comes on Monday," and she dragged again at his arm above the elbow.

"Where are we going?" he asked, holding back.

"Along to the kitchen. We've got a good ten minutes. Don't you want to see them caught?"

"No," he said, "no!" and pulled away from her.

'Mrs Driver stared at him, smiling a little. "I do," she said; "I'd like to see 'em close. He puffs this stuff in and they come running out. At least, that's how it works with rats. But first, he says, you have to block up all the exits…" and her eyes followed my brother's to the hole below the wainscot.

"How did they find it?" he asked then (puttied it looked, and with a square of brown paper pasted on crooked).

"Rich William found it. That's his job."

"They could unstick that," said the boy after a moment.

'Mrs Driver laughed—quite amiably for once. "Oh no they couldn't. Not now, they couldn't! Cemented, firm, that is. A great block of it, right inside, with a sheet of iron across from the front of that old stove in the outhouse. He and Crampfurl had to have the morning-room floor up to get at it. All Tuesday they was working, up till tea-time. We aren't going to have no more capers of that kind. Not under the clock. Once you get that clock back, it can't be moved again in a hurry. Not if you want it to keep time, it can't. See where it's stood—where the floor's washed away like?" It was then my brother saw, for the first and last time, that raised platform of unscrubbed stone. "Come on now," said Mrs Driver and took him by the arm. "We'll hear the cab from the kitchen."

'But the kitchen, as she dragged him past the baize door, seemed a babel of sound. No approaching cab could be heard here. "Steady, steady, steady, steady, steady…" Crampfurl was saying, on one loud note, as he held back the rat-catcher's terriers, which shrilled and panted on the leash. The policeman was there, Nellie Runacre's son Ernie. He had come out of interest and stood back from the others a little in view of his calling, with a cup of tea in his hand and his helmet pushed off his forehead. But his face was pink with boyish excitement and he stirred the teaspoon round and round. "Seeing's believing!" he said cheerfully to Mrs Driver when he saw her come in at the door. A boy from the village was there with a ferret. It kept sort of pouring out of his pocket, my brother said, and the boy kept pushing it back. Rich William himself was crouched on the floor by the hole. He had lighted something beneath a piece of sacking and the stench of its smouldering eddied about the room. He was working the bellows now, with infinite care, stooping over them—rapt and tense.

'My brother stood there as though in a dream ("Perhaps it was a dream," he said to me later—much later, after we were all grown up). He gazed round the kitchen. He saw the sunlit fruit trees through the window and a bough of the cherry-tree which stood upon the bank; he saw the empty tea-cups on the table, with spoons stuck in them and one without a saucer; he saw, propped against the wall close beside the baize door, the rat-catcher's belongings—a frayed coat, patched with leather; a bundle of rabbit snares; two sacks, a spade, a gun, and a pick-axe...

"Stand by now," Rich William was saying; there was a rising note of excitement in his voice, but he did not turn his head. "Stand by. Ready now to slip the dogs."

'Mrs Driver let go my brother's arm and moved towards the hole. "Keep back," said the rat-catcher, without turning.

"Give us room—" and Mrs Driver backed nervously towards the table. She put a chair beside it and half raised one knee, but lowered it again when she caught Ernie Runacre's mocking glance. "All right, ma," he said, cocking one eyebrow, "we'll give you a leg up when the time comes," and Mrs Driver threw him a furious look; she snatched up the three cups from the table and stumped away with them, angrily, in the direction of the scullery. "… seemingless smutch of something-or-other…" my brother heard her mutter as she brushed past him. And at those words, suddenly, my brother came to life…

'He threw a quick glance about the kitchen: the men were absorbed; all eyes were on the rat-catcher—except those of the village boy, who was getting out his ferret. Stealthily my brother drew off his gloves and began to move backwards… slowly… slowly… towards the green baize door; as he moved, gently stuffing his gloves into his pocket, he kept his eyes on the group around the hole. He paused a moment beside the rat-catcher's tools, and stretched out a wary, groping hand; his fingers closed at last on a wooden handle— smooth it was and worn with wear; he glanced down quickly to make sure—yes, it was, as he hoped, the pick-axe. He leaned back a little and pushed—almost imperceptibly— against the door with his shoulders: it opened sweetly, in its silent way. Not one of the men had looked up. "Steady now," the rat-catcher was saying, stooping closely over the bellows, "it takes a moment like to go right through… there ain't much ventilation, not under a floor…"

'My brother slid through the barely opened door and it sighed to behind him, closing out the noise. He took a few steps on tiptoe down the dark kitchen passage and then he ran.

'There was the hall again, steeped in sunshine, with his bags beside the door. He bumped against the clock and it struck a note, a trembling note—urgent and deep. He raised the pick-axe to the height of his shoulder and aimed a sideways blow at the hole below the wainscot. The paper tore, a few crumbs of plaster fell out, and the pick-axe rebounded sharply, jarring his hands. There was indeed iron behind the cement—something immovable. Again he struck. And again and again. The wainscot above the hole became split and scratched, and the paper hung down in strips, but still the pickaxe bounced. It was no good; his hands, wet with sweat, were sliding and slipping on the wood. He paused for breath and, looking out, he saw the cab. He saw it on the road, beyond the hedge on the far side of the orchard; soon it would reach the russet apple-tree beside the gate; soon it would turn into the drive. He glanced up at the clock. It was ticking steadily the result, perhaps, of his knock. The sound gave him comfort and steadied his thumping heart; time, that's what he needed, a little more time. "It takes a moment like," the rat-catcher had said, "to go right through… there ain't much ventilation, not under a floor…"

"Ventilation"—that was the word, the saving word. pick-axe in hand my brother ran out of the door. He stumbled once on the gravel path and nearly fell; the pick-axe handle came up and struck him a sharp blow on the temple. Already, when he reached it, a thin filament of smoke was eddying out of the grating and he thought, as he ran towards it, that there was a flicker of movement against the darkness between the bars. And that was where they would be, of course, to get the air. But he did not stop to make sure. Already he heard behind him the crunch of wheels on the gravel and the sound of the horse's hoofs. He was not, as I have told you, a very strong little boy, and he was only nine (not ten, as he had boasted to Arrietty) but, with two great blows on the brick-work, he dislodged one end of the grating. It fell down side-ways, slightly on a slant, hanging—it seemed—by one nail. Then he clambered up the bank and threw the pick-axe with all his might into the long grass beyond the cherry-tree. He remembered thinking as he stumbled back, sweaty and breathless, towards the cab, how that too—the loss of the pick-axe—would cause its own kind of trouble later.'

CHAPTER TWENTY

'But,' exclaimed Kate, 'didn't he see them come out?'

'No. Mrs Driver came along then, in a flurry of annoyance, because they were late for the train. She bustled him into the cab because she wanted to get back again, she said, as fast as she could to be "in at the death". Mrs Driver was like that.'

Kate was silent a moment, looking down.

'So that is the end,' she said at last.

'Yes,' said Mrs May, 'in a way: or the beginning...'

'But'—Kate raised a worried face—'perhaps they didn't escape through the grating? Perhaps they were caught after all?'

'Oh, they escaped all right,' said Mrs May lightly.

'But how do you know?'

'I just know,' said Mrs May.

'But how did they get across those fields? With the cows and things? And the crows?'

'They walked, of course. The Hendrearys did it. People can do anything when they have a mind to.'

'But poor Homily! She'd be so upset.'

'Yes, she was upset,' said Mrs May.

'And how would they know the way?'

'By the gas-pipe,' said Mrs May. 'There's a kind of ridge all along, through the spinney and across the fields. You see, when men dig a trench and put a pipe in it all the earth they've dug out doesn't quite fit when they've put it back. The ground looks different.'

'But poor Homily—she didn't have her tea or her furniture or her carpets or anything. Do you suppose they took anything?'

'Oh, people always grab something,' said Mrs May shortly, 'the oddest things sometimes—if you've read about shipwrecks.' She spoke hurriedly, as though she were tired of the subject. 'Do be careful, child—not grey next to pink. You'll have to unpick it.'

'But,' went on Kate in a despairing voice as she picked up the scissors, 'Homily would hate to arrive there all poor and desstute in front of Lupy.'

'Destitute,' said Mrs May patiently, 'and Lupy wasn't there, remember. Lupy never came back. And Homily would be in her element. Can't you see her? "Oh, these poor silly men…" she would cry and would tie on her apron at once.'

'Were they all boys?'

'Yes, Harpsichords and Clocks. And they'd spoil Arrietty dreadfully.'

'What did they eat? Did they eat caterpillars, do you think?'

'Oh, goodness, child, of course they didn't. They would have a wonderful life. Badgers' sets are almost like villages—full of passages and chambers and storehouses. They could gather hazel-nuts and beech-nuts and chestnuts; they could gather corn—which they could store and grind into flour, just as humans do—it was all there for them: they didn't even have to plant it. They had honey. They could make elderflower tea and lime tea. They had hips and haws and blackberries and sloes and wild strawberries. The boys could fish in the stream and a minnow to them would be as big as a mackerel is to you. They had birds' eggs—any amount of them—for custards and cakes and omelettes. You see, they would know where to look for things. And they had greens and salads, of course. Think of a salad made of those tender shoots of young hawthorn—bread and cheese we used to call it—with sorrel and dandelion and a sprinkling of thyme and wild garlic. Homily was a good cook remember. It wasn't for nothing that the Clocks had lived under the kitchen.'

'But the danger,' cried Kate; 'the weasels and the crows and the stoats and all those things?'

'Yes,' agreed Mrs May, 'of course there was danger. There's danger everywhere, but no more for them than for many of us. At least they didn't have *wars*. And what about the early settlers in America? And those people who farm in the middle of the big game country in Africa and on the edge of the jungles in India? They get to know the habits of the animals. Even rabbits know when a fox isn't hunting; they will run quite near when he's full fed and lazing in the sun. These were boys, remember; they would learn to hunt for the pot and how to protect themselves. I don't suppose it's very likely that Arrietty and Homily would wander far afield.'

'Arrietty would,' said Kate.

'Yes,' agreed Mrs May, laughing, 'I suppose Arrietty might.'

'So they'd have meat?' said Kate.

'Yes, sometimes. But Borrowers are Borrowers; not killers. I think,' said Mrs May, 'that if a stoat, say, killed a partridge they might borrow a leg!'

'And if a fox caught a rabbit they'd use the fur?'

'Yes, for rugs and things.'

'Supposing,' said Kate excitedly, 'when they had a little roast, they skinned haws and baked them, would they taste like browned potatoes?'

'Perhaps,' said Mrs May.

'But they couldn't cook in the badger's set. I suppose they cooked out of doors. How would they keep warm then in winter?'

'Do you know what I think?' said Mrs May; she laid down her work and leaned forward a little. 'I think that they didn't live in the badger's set at all. I think they used it, with all its passages and store-rooms, as a great honeycomb of an entrance hall. None but they would know the secret way through the tunnels which led at last to their home. Borrowers love passages and they love gates; and they love to live a long way from their own front doors.'

'Where *would* they live then?'

'I was wondering,' said Mrs May, 'about the gas-pipe—'

'Oh yes,' cried Kate, 'I see what you mean!'

'The soil's all soft and sandy up there. I think they'd go right through the badger's set and dig out a circular chamber, level with the gas-pipe. And off this chamber, all around it, there'd be little rooms, like cabins. And I think,' said Mrs May, 'that they'd bore three little pin-holes in the gas-pipe. One would be so tiny that you could hardly see it and that one would be always alight. The other two would have stoppers in them which, when they wanted to light the gas, they would pull out. They would light the bigger ones from the small burner. That's where they'd cook and that would give them light.'

'But would they be so clever?'

'But they are clever,' Mrs May assured her, 'very clever. Much too clever to live near a gas-pipe and not use it. They're Borrowers remember.'

'But they'd want a little air-hole?'

'Oh,' said Mrs May quickly, 'they did have one.'

'How do you know?' asked Kate.

'Because once when I was up there I smelled hot-pot.'

'Oh,' cried Kate excitedly; she twisted round and knelt up on the hassock, 'so you did go up there? So that's how you know! You saw them too!'

'No, no,' said Mrs May, drawing back a little in her chair, 'I never saw them. Never.'

'But you went up there? You know something! I can see

you know!'

'Yes, I went up there.' Mrs May stared back into Kate's eager face; hesitant, she seemed, almost a little guilty. 'Well,' she conceded at last, 'I'll tell you. For what it's worth. When I went to stay in that house it was just before Aunt Sophy went into the nursing home. I knew the place was going to be sold, so I'—again Mrs May hesitated, almost shyly—'well, I took all the furniture out of the doll's house and put it in a pillow-case and took it up there. I bought things too out of my pocket money—tea and coffee beans and salt and pepper and cloves and a great packet of lump sugar. And I took a whole lot of little pieces of silk which were over from making a patchwork quilt. And I took them some fish-bones for needles. I took the tiny thimble I had got in a Christmas pudding and a whole collection of scraps and cracker things I'd had in a chocolate box—'

'But you never saw them!'

'No. I never saw them. I sat for hours against the bank below the hawthorn hedge. It was a lovely bank, twined with twisted hawthorn roots and riddled with sandy holes and there were wood-violets and primroses and early campion. From the top of the bank you could see for miles across the fields: you could see the woods and the valleys and the twisting lanes; you could see the chimneys of the house.'

'Perhaps it was the wrong place.'

'I don't think so. Sitting there in the grass, half dreaming and watching beetles and ants, I found an oak-apple; it was smooth and polished and dry and there was a hole bored in one side of it and a slice off the top—'

'The teapot!' exclaimed Kate.

'I think so. I looked everywhere, but I couldn't find the quill spout. I called then, down all the holes—as my brother had done. But no one answered. Next day, when I went up there, the pillow case had gone.'

'And everything in it?'

'Yes, everything. I searched the ground for yards around, in case there might be a scrap of silk or a coffee bean. But there was nothing. Of course, somebody passing might just have picked it up and carried it away. That was the day,' said Mrs May, smiling, 'that I smelled hotpot.'

'And which was the day,' asked Kate, 'that you found Arrietty's diary?'

Mrs May laid down her work. 'Kate,' she began in a startled voice, and then, uncertainly, she smiled, 'what makes you say that?' Her cheeks had become quite pink.

'I guessed,' said Kate. 'I knew there was something— something you wouldn't tell me. Like—like reading somebody else's diary.'

'It wasn't the diary,' said Mrs May hastily, but her cheeks had become even pinker. 'It was the book called *Memoranda*, the book with blank pages. That's where she'd written it. And it wasn't on that day I found it, but three weeks later—the day before I left.'

Kate sat silent, staring at Mrs May. After a while she drew

a long breath. 'Then that proves it,' she said finally, 'underground chamber and all.'

'Not quite,' said Mrs May.

'Why not?' asked Kate.

'Arrietty used to make her "e's" like little half moons with a stroke in the middle—'

'Well?' said Kate.

Mrs May laughed and took up her work again. 'My brother did, too,' she said.